Ben Calder had made her aware of his masculinity within minutes,

and had made Maria aware of herself, too. She'd forgotten what it was like to have her heart beat when she met a man's eyes; she'd forgotten the way her skin could tingle when she stood close to a man. It felt strange to notice the hair on a man's arms, the strength of his fingers as he'd twisted that jar lid, to notice the beginning of five-o'clock shadow on a strong chin.

Strange, but very pleasant. It had just been so long. So long...

Dear Reader,

What better way for Silhouette Romance to celebrate the holiday season than to celebrate the meaning of family....

You'll love the way a confirmed bachelor becomes a FABULOUS FATHER just in time for the holidays in Susan Meier's *Merry Christmas, Daddy*. And in *Mistletoe Bride*, Linda Varner's HOME FOR THE HOLIDAYS miniseries merrily continues. The ugly duckling who becomes a beautiful swan will touch your heart in *Hometown Wedding* by Elizabeth Lane. Doreen Roberts's *A Mom for Christmas* tells the tale of a little girl's holiday wish, and in Patti Standard's *Family of the Year*, one man, one woman and a bunch of adorable kids form an unexpected family. And finally, *Christmas in July* by Leanna Wilson is what a sexy cowboy offers the struggling single mom he wants for his own.

Silhouette Romance novels make the perfect stocking stuffers—or special treats just for yourself. So enjoy all six irresistible books, and most of all, have a very happy holiday season and a very happy New Year!

Melissa Senate
Senior Editor
Silhouette Romance

Please address questions and book requests to:
Silhouette Reader Service
U.S.: 3010 Walden Ave., P.O. Box 1325, Buffalo, NY 14269
Canadian: P.O. Box 609, Fort Erie, Ont. L2A 5X3

FAMILY OF THE YEAR

Patti Standard

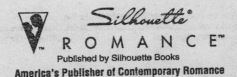

Silhouette®

ROMANCE™

Published by Silhouette Books

America's Publisher of Contemporary Romance

To Jim VanPelt and Walt Disney. Jim's class gave me the tools; Walt's videos gave me the time. And to Jean R. Ewing, a superb Regency romance author. Thanks for the sheep.

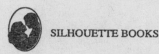 SILHOUETTE BOOKS

ISBN 0-373-19196-0

FAMILY OF THE YEAR

Copyright © 1996 by Patti Standard-Cronk

Printed in U.S.A.

Books by Patti Standard

Silhouette Romance

Pretty as a Picture #636
For Brian's Sake #829
Under One Roof #902
Family of the Year #1196

PATTI STANDARD

lives in one of the most beautiful spots in Colorado—
but can't seem to stay put. She loves to travel, and she
and her husband leave their engineering firm and take
off for parts unknown as often as they can get
Grandma to baby-sit. With three children, an assortment of pets, a yard with a life of its own, and a home
business where clients are forced to wade through the
remains of peanut butter and jelly sandwiches to get to
the office door, Patti needs regular vacations to keep
her romantic batteries charged. She's a die-hard
Trekkie with a mad crush on Captain Jean-Luc Picard,
and the heroes of her novels are always bald in the
first draft.

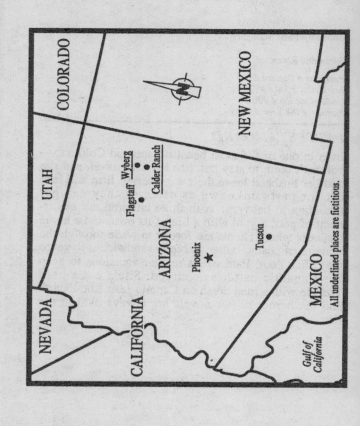

NEVADA

UTAH

COLORADO

CALIFORNIA

Flagstaff • Wyberg
• Calder Ranch

ARIZONA

Phoenix ★

NEW MEXICO

Tucson •

Gulf of
California

MEXICO

All underlined places are fictitious.

Chapter One

Benjamin Calder stood on the steps of the ranch house and looked down the driveway. He'd followed the roiling cloud of dust for the past few minutes, watching it turn off what passed for the main road and head toward the house. The cloud thinned and almost disappeared for a moment where the road ran through a stand of cottonwood trees down by the pond, only to reappear again near the fenced pasture. The billowing dust came close enough to separate out a car, something wide and vaguely green.

He looked at his watch, a wide silver band with an unpolished turquoise set on each side of the scratched face. It was almost four-thirty in the afternoon, just when she said she'd be there. Prompt. That was good. She must not have had any trouble on the way up from Phoenix. But Ben's guarded satisfaction with his new housekeeper was short-lived. The old station wagon came to a gravel-crunching stop in front of him and he caught a glimpse of the car's interior through the dusty windows. He was instantly wary.

The driver, dark hair tied back in a ponytail, had her head turned and was talking and gesturing toward the seats in back—seats that were filled with rows and rows of heads. Too many heads, Ben thought with a frown.

The engine tried to die, coughing and choking as if the long, gritty drive had robbed it of breath. Just as the last sputter sounded, the dented door at the rear of the station wagon swung open and out tumbled two dark-haired, wide-eyed little girls. The doors in the middle opened and a dark-haired boy ran to join them. From the other side, he saw a young woman emerge, a bundle carefully balanced in her arms. She rounded the car to stand beside the children and Ben's frown deepened as the bundle wiggled and a tiny arm began to bat at the air.

The passenger door opened next. An old woman, gray hair in a low bun, hoisted herself to her feet using the door's armrest and a thick, carved walking stick for leverage. She was still shuffling slowly over to join the rest of the group when the driver finally got out, her back to him. She stretched, arching her slender back and then rounding her shoulders inward, twisting her head from side to side while she tucked the end of a yellow blouse into her jeans.

She turned to face him. Dark haired and olive skinned like the rest, slim, not much taller than the look-alike children, with brown eyes that took up her whole face, she moved to the front of the too-silent group. She squared her shoulders and lifted her chin. She took on a dignity that belied the dented old car and the tired lines around those magnificent eyes.

"I am Maria Soldata," she announced.

"Benjamin Calder," he replied, nodding his head in what amounted to almost a bow, unconsciously reacting to the measured formality of her tone.

"This is my family." Another formal, grand statement as if the exhausted group surrounding her were being presented at court. "My mother, Juanita Romero." The old lady graciously inclined her head. "My sister, Veronica, and her baby, Ashley." The girl smiled, a beautiful young woman, but pale and tired looking. "This is my nephew, David, and my daughters, Tina and Trisha." The children just stared up at him and he stared back, not bothering to remember their names. After all, they couldn't be staying here long enough for it to matter—not all of them, anyway.

"Is that the guest house?" She looked inquiringly in the direction of the small, white-stuccoed building beside the main house.

"Yes, it is. But—"

But Maria Soldata had already turned, and the group turned with her. They dived back into the station wagon, all but the pretty girl whose arms were already full. They emerged simultaneously, hauling brown paper sacks that overflowed with food, dragging battered suitcases and boxes. The little boy, arms thin as matchsticks, struggled to lift a cardboard box with a sagging bottom. Ben was forced to hurry down the steps to help him before the bottom gave way completely and spilled what appeared to be an assortment of baby paraphernalia all over the gravel driveway.

He found himself, box in hand, with no choice but to follow Maria into the guest house while scurrying children flowed around him. Back and forth between the car and the house they went, each time their little arms straining with a load. And through it all, Maria's voice, making it impossible for him to get a word in edgewise.

"David, you take that bed. Girls, you take that one." She pointed through the open door to the two single beds in the small bedroom. "Mama and Veronica, you share the big bed." She gestured to the double bed visible in the main bedroom. She handed a child the folding cot she had tucked under one arm. "Set this up for me against that wall over there, please, Trisha." She rescued a portable bassinet the other girl was dragging over the threshold. "Thank you, sweetheart. Let me take that for you. We'll put the baby in with Aunt Veronica and *abuela,* okay? Such a good helper!" She disappeared into the room only to reappear in an instant.

"Bedding?"

Ben was surprised to find himself addressed. He stood in the middle of the kitchen, still holding the box of baby things. He glanced toward the pantry closet door and started to speak, but she was already there. She pulled the door open and took down a stack of linens. Grimly, he closed his mouth.

"Girls, help your *abuela* make up the beds, please, and then I want all you kids in the bath." She divided the stack between two waiting sets of arms, pausing only long enough to give each sweaty forehead a quick push-aside of bangs in a maternal caress.

"Veronica, can you—" But a loud squall from the bundle in the girl's arms stopped her. "Never mind. Why don't you hop in the tub with the baby now. You'll both feel better once you're cooled off and she's fed. Maybe after you've gotten her to sleep you can help Mama get supper? There's hot dogs and pork 'n' beans." Quick kisses all the way around and Maria was heading out the door. "I've got to get Mr. Calder's supper now and then I'll be back to put you kids to bed. Love you." She paused at the open door, a shadow outlined by the setting sun behind her.

"Mr. Calder? Coming?"

Ben sat the box on the kitchen table, feeling uncharacteristically overwhelmed. Damn that Vergie, anyway, he cursed his recently departed housekeeper. This was all her fault.

He'd begged her, pleaded with her. He remembered the conversation they'd had in this very room.

"You aren't really going to do this to me, are you?" Ben had watched his housekeeper calmly pack the suitcase on her bed. "I mean, Pakistan? Can't you save children around Wyberg or somewhere closer to home?" Vergie Mc-Phearson had simply added another pair of new, khaki-colored pants to the suitcase. "How about over on the reservation? Can't you vaccinate kids there? Do you even know how to give shots?"

"They'll teach me," Vergie told him, her voice firm. "Mildred went to Bangladesh last year through this same relief agency and she said they'll teach us everything we need to know." Ben tried to imagine her and Mildred Swanson, both fiftyish and almost-fat, in a barren desert tent with rows of veiled mothers and naked babies—but he couldn't do it. She'd been his housekeeper for three years and he'd never even seen her in a pair of pants!

She closed the suitcase with a click of finality. "Now, I'll be back the last week of August." She pushed around his frowning bulk to gather things from the dresser top and pile them into a blue nylon carryon. "A summer on your own won't be so bad."

"But it's not on my own. You're forgetting Connor will be here in less than two weeks."

"The freezers are jammed and TV dinners aren't so bad these days. You can manage those. And there won't be much laundry with just the two of you. Try to remember to separate the whites and use bleach on them or your underwear will all be gray by the time I get back."

The long, zipping sound of the closing carryall made Ben's stomach sink. "What about the garden? The canning?"

"Mr. Calder, you've known about my trip for two months now." Vergie sounded exasperated. "Maybe you can get somebody from Wyberg to come out a few times a week."

"I've tried. Nobody wants to drive sixty miles one way just to can my tomatoes."

"I told you to try Phoenix, then," Vergie reminded him. "You could let somebody stay here." She indicated the guest house with a sweep of her hand, setting the loose skin on the pale underside of her arm jiggling. "I wouldn't mind somebody using my stuff for a while."

"Who would want to move up here for a job that'll only last for three months? I don't want some college kid on summer vacation."

"You never know. Phoenix gets mighty hot in the summer. Here—" Vergie handed him a notepad and pen from beside the telephone "—you write up an ad and I'll phone it in to the newspapers down there before I go. If you said 'Family OK' you might get some nice single mother. That'd do the trick."

Ben had stared at the blank paper in his hand. He envisioned a summer of TV dinners, vacuuming, ripening tomatoes . . . and Connor. A father shouldn't feel such dread at the thought of seeing his son, he knew, but he couldn't help it. Six weeks alone with a sullen seventeen-year-old and a boom box? He'd grasped the pen, lips tight with determination, and began to write.

And this is where it'd landed him, he thought with consternation as he followed the back of his new housekeeper across the driveway, up the wide stairs, across the porch and into his house. She hesitated only a moment in the doorway before heading unerringly in the direction of the kitchen.

"Well, Mr. Calder, what would you like for supper tonight? Do you have something already planned?" She stuck her hands under running water at the sink and soaped them with the bar next to the faucet. "Will it be just you tonight or do you have hired hands who eat with you? Do you—"

"Stop!" Ben slammed down the faucet lever. Maria jumped and then froze, hands still covered with soap. She looked up at him, dark eyes huge. Damn, he hadn't meant to bellow like that! And here he was, towering over her, her head no higher than his shoulder. No wonder she'd jumped out of her skin. But Benjamin Calder, fourth generation owner of Calder Ranch, was used to being in charge of a situation, and so far his new housekeeper had treated him pretty much as if he was just one more of that passel of people out in his guest house. It was time to get to the bottom of this.

Maria held her breath. Here it came. He was going to send them packing. She ached, stiff and sore from the long drive up in the heat, the last twenty miles over a washboard dirt road that jarred the very teeth from her head. Her temples pounded from hours in a cramped car listening to children fight in the back. And now this man, the man who had the power to send them back to the purgatory that was Phoenix in the summer, had her pushed up against a sink—and didn't look as if he planned to move anytime soon.

Benjamin Calder was big—tall and broad shouldered. He wore faded jeans and a denim work shirt with the sleeves rolled up away from his wrists. Every inch of visible skin was richly tanned and a sweat-stained cowboy hat covered dark brown hair. From hat to scuffed leather boots, he was sifted with a fine layer of the reddish dust that made up the earth in this part of Arizona, a dust that Maria could already feel on her, gritting between her teeth and itching in her nose. His physical presence was overpowering enough; it didn't help that he glowered down at her, thick eyebrows joined to form a forbidding slash across his forehead.

"All those people out there—" he jerked his head in the direction of the window "—are they visiting?"

Maria slowly, consciously, let out her breath and tried to school her features into a look of innocence. "I guess you could say that. Sort of a three-month visit."

"Now just hold on here! When I talked to you on the phone, you never mentioned—"

"The ad said 'Family OK,'" Maria interrupted. Quickly, she wiped her soapy hands on a rag and dug into the pocket of her jeans. She pulled out a folded scrap of newsprint and smoothed it open. "Look. 'Household help needed for summer on ranch sixty miles outside of Wyberg. Hard work. Family OK.'"

"But I meant—"

"I specifically asked you on the phone—"

"But I didn't mean—"

"And you specifically said it was all right to bring up my family."

"I meant a kid or two. Not a station wagon full."

"They're my family," Maria said simply. "I promise you, they won't be any trouble at all. My mother and my sister will watch the children while I work. We've brought our own food, we won't be any bother and we won't cost you any extra."

But Ben shook his head, making fine red dust motes sparkle in the afternoon sun coming through the kitchen window. "It won't do."

"Come on, now," Maria chided, "what do you want for supper?" She shifted and reached out to turn on the water.

"I said it won't do!" He grabbed her hand and spun her around.

They stood facing each other, eyes locked, his hand still on hers, wills engaged in a battle without words. Maria was uncomfortably aware of the breadth of him as he stood so close. He smelled of horse and sage and leather, male smells foreign to her city senses. His eyes were as gray as the haze against the mountains on a summer afternoon, and, even full of anger, they reflected an instinctive, masculine awareness of her.

She tried to pull her fingers from his grip, but her efforts were laughable. Although not painful, the calloused hardness of his hand only emphasized her fragile position. The silence lengthened. The fine dust spun between them, dancing on unseen currents. It was finally too much for her; her nose twitched, twitched again . . . and she sneezed, a short, sharp achoo.

Maria stared at Ben. In the startled silence that followed, the rumble of his stomach was very audible, long and distinct, fading away slowly like distant thunder.

Her laugh joined with his snort of mirth. He dropped her hand and moved back a step.

Maria smiled. "I tell you what, let me make you some supper and get the children a good night's sleep, all right? Then we'll see about being out of your hair in the morning."

"Sounds fair." He nodded, looking relieved. "Sorry for the misunderstanding."

"That's all right. No hard feelings."

She moved to the refrigerator and peered inside, seemingly intent on its well-stocked contents, but Ben had seen the white lines of tension that had appeared around her mouth in spite of her smile and accepting words. As for there being no hard feelings, the look that had come into those expressive Mexican eyes was as close to panic as Ben Calder had ever seen.

"Are those crickets, Mama?" Tina asked, snuggling back between her mother's open knees as they sat on the porch steps of the little guest house and listened to the sounds of a desert night.

"I think so." Maria continued her rhythmic brushing of the little girl's hair, the repetitive motion soothing to them both.

"They sound awfully loud for crickets. They aren't so loud in Phoenix."

"They get drowned out by the sirens." Juanita Romero's voice creaked through the darkness, drier even than the creaking of the rocking chair she kept in motion with an occasional nudge of her walking stick against the wooden floorboards.

Trisha, Maria's oldest daughter, looked up at the night sky, her head tilted so far back her long hair touched the step behind her. "And there's a lot more stars up here, did you notice that, Mama?"

"I think you might be right." Maria's eyes filled with a sudden rush of tears. She wanted crickets for her children. She wanted stars. They had to stay, there *must* be a way.

"Mama, not so hard! You're hurting me," Tina tried to pull her head away from Maria's unintentional increase in pressure.

"Sorry, sweetheart." Sighing, Maria resumed the gentle movement. Of course Mr. Calder was right, she admitted to herself. She knew she was stepping over the line to bring everyone up here and foist them on him. But what choice had she had? She was still haunted by that look on Veronica's face that horrible morning last week. The cool evening around her faded, replaced by the interior of her Phoenix apartment, as Maria remembered.

"He's gone." Veronica had wearily leaned her head back against the top of the sofa, her dark hair fanning out to cover the worn spot in the avocado tweed. The baby she held in her arms listlessly nuzzled her breast, too hot to suckle.

"Tucson isn't exactly the ends of the earth, you know." Maria had tried her best to keep her tone low and soothing, both for her sister's sake and not to disturb the fussy infant, quieted for the first time that morning.

"He won't be back." Veronica's voice was as flat as her dark eyes. "I'm surprised he hasn't bolted sooner. This family doesn't have the best luck keeping men around."

Maria's lips turned up in a mirthless smile of agreement.

"He said the job's just for the summer, but I know he'll keep right on going." Veronica shifted, trying to pull her blouse away from her sweat-sticky back. The movement caused the baby to let out a wail of protest and Veronica froze, then carefully leaned back against the sofa again. Both women let out a sigh of relief when the baby began to nurse. "Roberto loves you," Maria insisted. "And you both agreed that he couldn't pass up this job. You'll need that money for his tuition this fall."

God, she looks so tired, Maria thought as she watched her sister, pale and gaunt, run a finger along the rhythmically moving cheek of her infant daughter. The pregnancy had been very hard on her, and it hadn't helped that she'd worked right up to the day she delivered, long shifts on her feet at the family's restaurant. Maria still winced, remembering the sight of her sister's swollen ankles.

She wished she could offer her some reassurance. Roberto *did* love her. But their first year of marriage had been difficult, marrying so soon after graduation and getting pregnant almost immediately. When Roberto's uncle had offered him a summer job in Tucson at wages too good to turn down, he'd jumped at it.

For her sister's sake, Maria had to believe he'd be back, in spite of the way his phone calls had suddenly stopped and Veronica's letters went unanswered. Although, as Veronica had said, there'd hardly been a man in the family so far who'd stuck around. Was Roberto, barely twenty years old, going to be more responsible and mature than the rest?

"You know Linda's losing her apartment?" Veronica asked.

Maria nodded at the mention of their older sister. "Mama told me they're turning her building into condos. I said she could stay here while she's looking for a new place but I don't know where we're going to put David. I hate to put him in the same room with the girls. It'd be hell trying to get three kids to sleep at night."

"And he's so hyper. He's been giving Linda fits. Ever since his dad took off, it's been one thing after another."

They listened in silence while the swamp cooler growled ineffectively at the heat. Maria watched the water leaking around the edges of the old machine run down the wallpaper and drip into the pan on the floor, a faint round rust stain on the vinyl marking the exact spot for it.

"I guess I should get going. I told Mama I'd be home for lunch." But Veronica made no move to rise.

Maria felt the sweat that had pooled behind her knees begin to trickle down the backs of her legs. She wiped at it with her hands, then rubbed her hands against her shorts. "I'll fix you something, if you want." Maria knew she sounded almost as lethargic as her sister, stupefied by the heat.

"I hate Phoenix in the summer." But Veronica seemed unable to put any emotion into the words. "It's supposed to get up to one hundred and five today."

The noise of Maria's girls squabbling in their bedroom began to grow more insistent and a siren rose somewhere outside. It would be nice to be able to leave Phoenix in the summer like most of their customers did, Maria thought. With college out, their little family restaurant was nearly empty most evenings, and not only was time hanging heavy but bills were mounting. Even a quick weekend up to Flag-staff was out of the question.

Little Tina came bursting into the room, waving a doll with long blond hair, her sister in hot pursuit. "Mama, I had it first! Tell her it's mine! It's mine!" Maria was engulfed by crying, angry girls, the awakened baby began to wail and the siren in the background got louder and closer.

Get out! something inside Maria screamed. *I've got to get out!* The words went around and around in her brain as she fought for a gulp of cool air in the stifling apartment. *I have to get my family out of here!*

Maria started, brought back to the present by Tina's impatient wiggling. She resumed her brushing, staring into the dark over her daughter's head. That ad in the paper had been like a sign. She would have said anything, agreed to anything, to get the job. Three months out here away from the city, with nothing but sandstone and sagebrush and fresh air and hard work—it was just what they all needed, adults as well as kids. She had to find a way to make Mr. Calder see it would work out.

But Maria remembered the way he'd glared at her in the kitchen, that stubborn look of a man used to getting his own way in eyes the same gray as the sage all around. Benjamin Calder had said no. Politely, yet firmly.

Maria listened to the incredible richness of sound of the quiet country night, surrounded by her family, all safe and happy for the time being. Benjamin Calder might have said no, she told herself, but Benjamin Calder was a man. And for Maria Soldata and the women she knew, men were something to be worked around, something to ignore as much as possible—something to survive in spite of.

The sound of laughter drew Ben to the kitchen window that looked out on the guest house. He walked over, shirt pulled out of his jeans and unbuttoned to the waist, and turned slightly so he could see through the crack in the sheer white curtains.

Two of the children tumbled about on the grass at the edge of the porch, somersaulting themselves dizzy. The old woman rocked in the chair Vergie always sat in to do her knitting, just a silhouette in the evening shadows. The girl was in the porch swing, her hand keeping up a steady patting motion against the back of the baby she held to her shoulder.

His about-to-be-ex-housekeeper, Maria Soldata, who had just finished fixing him the best meal he'd eaten in two weeks, brushed the hair of one of the little girls, Tony or Tiny or something like that, spotlighted by the yellow light coming through the open door behind them. He watched her hands move. First the stroke of the brush with one hand, followed by a smoothing caress of the other hand— smoothing, stroking, smoothing, stroking.

Their voices drifted across to him, low and indistinguishable, an occasional word of Spanish spicing the sound. Family talk. Ben thought of Connor, who should be there in two more days. Family.

He reached out to flip off the light switch and stood there in the darkened kitchen. He knew that the feeling that gripped him, held him by the window, was envy.

Ben woke to the smell of bacon and fresh coffee, the aroma tantalizing his eyes open. He rolled over and looked at the clock. Five-thirty. Damn that woman, anyway! That wasn't playing fair. How'd she know he'd been eating cold cereal for the past two weeks?

He picked his jeans off the floor, swatted them a few times to try to remove some of the dust and pulled them on. They were his last clean pair—or least dirty pair, anyway.

Thankfully, he still had a couple of clean work shirts in the closet. He took one from the hanger and shrugged into it, then picked up yesterday's from the foot of the bed. Struggling into his boots, he took the shirt down the hall to the laundry room to add it to the overflowing basket.

Except the basket wasn't overflowing anymore. The washer hummed and the dryer purred and neatly folded stacks of clean clothes covered both surfaces. Damn that woman, anyway. How'd she know this was his last pair of clean socks?

The spotless living room, two weeks' worth of newspapers gone from the coffee table, annoyed him even further, and when he heard the sound of laughter coming from the kitchen... that was the last straw. How'd she know how much he hated waking up to a silent, empty house?

He stomped into the kitchen and glared at Maria and the man at his table.

"Morning, boss," Harvey Wainright, his hired hand, greeted him, happily downing a plate of eggs and hash browns.

"It won't work," Ben announced, ignoring Harvey.

"So you said." Maria indicated the table with the coffeepot she held in her hand and left the stove to pour him a cup. "How do you want your eggs?"

Grimly, he sat down in front of the steaming cup. "Sunny-side up."

"That's not good for you anymore, you know. What with salmonella in the chickens these days, you need to cook your eggs more. I'll make them over-easy."

"I said sunny-side up." There she went again! Completely ignoring him just like last night, as if he was of no account. "Those eggs come from *my* chickens and *my* chickens don't have salmonella and I'll eat them *raw* if I want to!"

"Easy there, boss," Harvey said, his faded eyes opening wide in surprise. "You know, I read about that salmonella thing a while back. You can't be too careful. And Maria makes darned good over-easy." He smiled his gap-toothed smile at Maria.

"That's okay, Harvey. If he grows his own chickens, then I'm sure sunny-side up will be perfectly all right."

"You don't *grow* chickens. You *raise* chickens," Ben mumbled into his cup, annoyed by Harvey's good mood. Frowning, he watched Maria crack the eggs into the pan, making the melted butter sizzle.

"It wasn't necessary to do all this, you know," he addressed her back. "Since it's not going to work out, I mean."

"It wasn't any trouble."

"I'll pay you for your time so far."

"That's not necessary."

"I insist." He leaned forward to take his checkbook from the back pocket of his jeans.

Maria made no further protest. She slid the eggs from the pan onto the waiting plate, added a scoop of hash browns, some bacon and four pieces of buttered toast.

Ben propped the check next to the saltshaker, then began to eat in moody silence, only half listening to Harvey. His eyes strayed often to Maria as she cleaned up the kitchen.

When the clock reached six, Ben scraped back his chair and stood. "It's time to get to work. I won't be back to the house till noon so I guess I'll say goodbye now. You'll probably want to head out while it's still cool."

"All right. Goodbye."

"Goodbye. Thanks for the meals and the laundry and all."

Maria nodded.

"Anyway, uh, thanks." Why did he feel as if he should apologize? The last thing he needed was a pack of kids running all over the place and a crying baby and a mean-looking old woman.

"Nice meeting you, Maria." Harvey bobbed his grizzled head and the two men headed out the kitchen door, letting the screen door slam behind them.

"She did your laundry?" Maria could hear Harvey's voice through the open window as they walked across the yard to the corral.

"Shut up, Harvey."

"Real good cook."

"Shut up, Harvey."

"Pretty little thing, too."

"I said shut up, Harvey."

"Lot easier on your eyes than old Vergie, the viper-tongued, rat-eyed..." Their voices faded away in the distance.

Maria finished the last of the dishes and went outside. The morning was glorious, golden and clean. She stopped with her hand on the doorknob to the guest house and turned around, surveying the red hills in the distance. Huge cottonwoods ringed the house in a circle of shade, the only sound the wind in their leaves, the clucking of chickens somewhere nearby, the faraway barking of a dog.

She pushed open the door and clapped her hands sharply together; the sound shot through the silent rooms. "Up and at 'em!" She moved into the bedroom and began jiggling sleeping bodies, pulling back warm covers. "Up, everybody. It's time to get to work!"

Ben swore as he bounced his pickup into the yard and came to a stop next to the green station wagon that was supposed to have been on its way back to Phoenix hours ago. He peered through the dusty windows, but the cracked vinyl seats were empty—no boxes, bags or packed suitcases. Damn, damn and double damn!

He took the porch stairs two at a time and strode through the door. His nose was immediately assaulted by the sickening-sweet smell of lemon polish, and his first step of booted foot on the throw rug sent him skidding, bucking across the mirror-smooth floor like he was riding a bull, his arms windmilling wildly for balance. He regained his footing with an ignominious grab for the coatrack, aimed a few choice words at the offending rug, then gave it a vicious kick back toward the door. It sailed effortlessly across the newly polished wooden boards to land in a wrinkled pile of woven cotton cowering against the doorjamb.

The smell of lemon wax gave way to the bite of bleach as he passed the open door to the bathroom. He smelled tomatoes as he stormed into the kitchen, bellowing for Maria. A pot of tomato soup simmered on the stove and a plate of sandwiches towered on the table, reflecting light off the clear plastic wrap protecting them. His check remained where he'd left it next to the salt.

"Maria!" he shouted again. Impatiently, Ben pulled back the curtain over the sink that looked out on the garden and the guest house.

He stared in dismay at the sight that greeted him. His garden had sprouted more than zucchini, it seemed. Three small children were on their knees, a growing pile of weeds beside each little figure. Veronica bent over the green beans, tying their slender tendrils to a string stretched above them. Maria had a hoe in her hands and steadily and methodically struck it into the ground around the ankle-high corn, neatly slicing the offending weeds out at the root. Ben watched her, fascinated by the smooth movement of her muscles as she swung the hoe, the strength in her long, tanned legs in their cutoff shorts, the way her bare toes dug into the dirt.

It was after one o'clock and the sun was high overhead and hot enough to have even the old lady, rocking in the shade with the baby propped against her ample stomach, wiping at her forehead. It was hard, backbreaking work he watched, yet all he heard was... happiness. High, childish voices made a nonstop background to the women's talk, an occasional reprimand from one of them as a small hand mistook a plant for a weed, the squeals and coos of the contented baby.

And he was going to send them packing.

Another sound made itself heard, a jarring, out-of-place sound that ripped through the hot summer afternoon. It was an engine, open full throttle and roaring in protest; it was the sickening, tearing sound of a too-low undercarriage scraping over a high spot in the dirt road; it was the squeal of brakes and spraying of gravel.

Ben went out the kitchen door, not daring the slippery living room again. A sinking feeling grew in his stomach as he anticipated what he would find. He rounded the corner of the house and there, in his driveway, was a brand-new, shiny red convertible, its radio blasting out the annoying, repetitive beat of rap. Leaping from the car, not bothering to open the door, was his son, Connor Calder.

"Hey, Dad! What do you think? Isn't she great?" Connor's chest stuck out so far his shoulder blades almost touched in back as he preened in front of his car.

"She's great, son." Ben tried to swallow his dismay at his son's day-early arrival. He saw the children appear and sidle up beside him. Their grandmother came, too, walking with heavy, slow steps, a baby in one arm and stick in the other. All were curious to see what caused the commotion. And there was Maria. They formed a warm, protective wall behind him, an insulating presence that helped absorb some of the roar and the rap and the blinding glare of the red sports car.

"Connor, I'd like you to meet Maria Soldata. She's my housekeeper for the summer. And this is her family—they'll be staying with her."

Chapter Two

"Hey." The boy's bored, insolent greeting was accompanied by a flick of his head to move long brown bangs out of his eyes. They were the same sage gray as his father's, Maria noticed. She wondered at the stiffness of the man beside her, and wondered even more at his sudden change of heart in letting them stay, and she wondered most of all what this boy had to do with it.

Suddenly, Connor snapped to attention. *"Chaqui-i-i-ta!"* he drawled. "Who's the babe?"

Maria followed the boy's eyes and saw that Veronica had joined the group. Barefoot, wiping her hands on her shorts, she looked young and lovely.

"Could you please turn off that music so we don't have to shout," Ben asked.

"Sure, man, chill out." Connor leaned over inside the car and flipped a knob. "So who's the hot tamale over there?"

Maria saw Ben's fingers curl into his palm, making a fist tight enough to turn his knuckles white. He looked as if his hand itched with the need to connect with the seat of his son's hole-filled jeans.

"This *young lady* is Veronica, Maria's sister." Ben stared pointedly at the boy. "And *young ladies* are to be spoken to with respect."

"Respect. Absolutely. In fact, I think I've died and gone to heaven—respectfully." Connor's reverent gaze was fixed on Veronica.

Veronica rolled her eyes, but Maria saw the faint blush on her cheeks and the beginning of a smile she tried to suppress. Obviously, what sounded obnoxious to Maria didn't strike her younger sister quite that way.

"I wasn't expecting you until tomorrow," Ben said.

"Mom and Mike got me the wheels yesterday for my birthday." He ran his hand lovingly along the door. "Man, it's great having a stepdad who owns a car dealership, ain't it? Oh, thanks for the check, too. I used it to get these mag beauties here. Great, huh?" Connor pulled his eyes from Veronica and leaned over to admire himself in one of the chrome wheels, frowning for a moment at the layer of dust it had accumulated. "Anyway, now that I'm mobile, I wanted a chance to test it out—so, here I am."

With the self-centeredness of youth always sure of a welcome, he walked past his father and over to Veronica. "If you're ever in the market for a car, I've got connections. I can get you something really sweet." He flipped his bangs.

"I'll keep that in mind," Veronica said dryly.

"Want to go for a spin?"

"No, thanks. I've got work to do."

"Not me. I'm on vacation. Take a rain check on that ride, okay?" Connor persisted.

"We'll see."

"Right. Let's plan on checking out Wyberg this evening." Brashly assuming he'd just made a date, Connor headed toward the front door. "I'm starved. Got anything to eat?"

"Connor, don't you have any bags?" Ben asked. Maria blinked at the dark tone of Ben's voice, but the boy didn't seem to notice.

"They're in the trunk. I'll get 'em later. Or let the help bring 'em up."

"Connor!"

All eyes swung to Ben as his voice thundered out, and Maria found three children pressed close against her legs.

"All right, already. I'll get the bags." Connor loped back off the porch and pressed the trunk release on the car, lifting out a bulging duffel bag and a backpack. "Lighten up, Dad. You're going to have a heart attack. You probably have a cholesterol count through the roof with all those eggs you eat." With a toss of bangs, Connor bounded up the stairs and into the house, leaving the door hanging open behind him.

Maria felt sorry for Ben as she saw him take a deep breath to try and regain control. A contrast of anger and embarrassment chased across his face, but his eyes—his eyes remained constant. His eyes were bleak.

"Those weeds are growing inches while we stand here, kids. Better get back to work." Maria tried to sound as if the scene she'd just witnessed was nothing out of the ordinary. She gave the children little pushes in the direction of the garden. "Go with Aunt Veronica and let's see if we can finish up before afternoon cartoons come on." Glad to get away from the tension they didn't understand, the children ran, shouting and whooping around the corner of the house, followed by their aunt and very disapproving-looking grandmother. Maria was left alone with Ben.

They looked at each other for a moment. "I guess we're staying, then?" Maria asked quietly.

"Please."

One word, but said so fervently, Maria couldn't help but wonder as she watched Benjamin Calder turn and walk into his house, closing behind him the door his son had left gaping open.

Ben stood at the stove, ladling out a bowl of soup. The plate of sandwiches had disappeared. Maria entered the kitchen and, without comment, went to the refrigerator, took out a plate of sliced meat and calmly began to fix more sandwiches.

Ben appreciated the silence and he appreciated the calm. He appreciated the two big sandwiches Maria sat on the table beside him a few moments later. He appreciated the way she went about gathering ingredients from the pantry and set to making what appeared to be the crust for a peach cobbler, her movements quick and efficient and without fuss.

"Do you know how to can?"

Maria seemed surprised by his sudden question. She made a moue of distaste while she worked at removing the ring from a quart jar of home-canned peaches. "I know how."

"But you don't like it?"

"It's not that I don't like it, it's just that—" She paused, holding her breath while she exerted pressure once again on the jar, twisting at the circle of metal.

"Just what?" He got up and took the jar from her, closed a broad hand around its neck and twisted. "There." He handed it back to her. "We do a lot of canning here."

"Thanks." She dumped the golden halves into a bowl and began to slice them. "Have you ever heard of gleaning?"

Ben shook his head and leaned against the countertop beside her, watching her fish the peaches from the thick syrup and deftly slice them into the waiting pan.

"In Phoenix, they have this government program where they let us go into the fields after the picking machines have gone through. You can have—free—whatever is left, the too-small vegetables, the imperfect stuff, as much as you can carry out. Doesn't matter what it is—green beans, pumpkins, tomatoes—you fill as many bushel baskets as you can fit in your car, then you drag them home and you can nonstop for however many days it takes before the stuff begins to spoil." Maria stopped and searched in the cupboard above her head for the cinnamon. "So, anyway," she continued, measuring into a spoon, "it's not that I don't like to can, it's more that I have unpleasant memories of the process."

"Umm." Ben nodded, showing his understanding without comment. But he thought about what it must be like for a woman like Maria to have to stand in the middle of a field in the Phoenix sun, probably surrounded by those same children out in his garden right now, to lug somebody else's leftovers into that old station wagon, to know that you had days of canning over steaming kettles to look forward to. To know that you had to do it if you wanted to feed your children during the upcoming winter.

"I'm afraid the cherries will be ready any day," he told her apologetically.

But she merely nodded. "I'll be ready, too, then. What other chores are there?"

"Well, have you ever gathered eggs?"

"You mean those salmonella-free eggs that you can eat raw? I'm afraid not."

Ben laughed out loud and, with a conscious effort, let his worries about Connor slip to the back of his mind.

"There's not much to it. It'll take about a week to figure out all the hens' hiding places, then all you do is check every morning and gather up what you find."

"Sounds easy enough. The kids will probably get a kick out of doing it." Maria unfolded the waiting crust over the fruit and began pinching the edges. "What else?"

"Mostly normal household chores, cooking, cleaning—you seem to have no problem with those things. Then there's the garden—which you're on top of. We're pretty self-sufficient with most things. The freezers are full of Calder Ranch meat and we have our own milk cows."

Maria looked up at him doubtfully. "Milk cows?"

"Don't worry." He smiled. "Harvey takes care of the milking morning and night. But you will have to skim off the cream and we do make our own butter."

"You're kidding!" Maria looked around the kitchen as if searching for anything resembling what she thought a churn might look like.

But Ben pointed to the food processor shining powerfully in a corner of the counter. "You pour it in there, hit the button, go do a load of laundry or something and when you come back, presto! Butter. You add a little salt, pat it into shape—" Ben made a snowball-making motion with his hands "—wrap it in some plastic and throw it in the freezer. That's all there is to it."

"Hmmm." Maria still looked skeptical. "I don't have to bake bread, do I?"

"Do you know how?"

Maria nodded.

"Well, as much as I love fresh-baked bread, I don't expect that." He pushed away from the counter. "Follow me." He waited while Maria slid the cobbler into the heated oven, then led her into the large pantry off of the kitchen. "I don't know if you had a chance to explore in here yet, but I think you'll find enough to feed a small army." He walked over to the three freezers lining one wall and lifted the lid on each, leaving them propped open for her to peer in.

"Wow!" Maria exclaimed. One freezer was completely filled with meat, identical white-wrapped packages with words printed in black marker identifying the contents. One freezer contained fruits and vegetables, and the last freezer had several dozen loaves of store-bought bread, homemade pies and cakes and enough TV dinners to last for months.

"Didn't you tell Vergie I knew how to cook?" Maria asked, indicating the alphabetically stacked TV dinners.

"Vergie believes in being well-prepared for any emergency." He gave each lid a push closed. "I know it looks like a lot but we're pretty isolated here in the winter. The main road is a mess when it snows so we try not to go into town more than once every couple of weeks or so."

They went back to the kitchen. "I don't think you'll have any trouble getting the hang of things," Ben told her. "But you be sure to ask if you need anything." He looked down at her standing beside him and frowned as he realized again just how small she was in spite of the way she'd wielded the hoe in the garden. "It's hard work, you know."

"Vergie managed."

"She's strong as an ox."

"When's the last time you spent a summer in Phoenix?"

"You couldn't pay me enough," Ben said flatly.

"Exactly. This is going to be like a summer vacation for me."

Just then the kitchen began to reverberate with the pulsing thrum of music coming from above their heads; the bass notes throbbed so violently Ben could feel them through the soles of his feet.

"Ah, yes, summer vacation." Ben sighed, deep and heavy.

Maria smiled. "I guess I better help the kids finish the garden," she said. "I'll get them some supper, then I'll be back to fix something for you and Connor. What time do you usually eat?''

"I try to finish up outside by six-thirty or so, so I have time to do my paperwork in the evenings." A particularly intense beat caused the dishes to rattle in the cupboards. "Uh, I was just thinking," Ben added casually, "why don't you plan on eating supper with us from now on?"

Maria shook her head. "Thanks, but I like to be with my girls for meals.''

"Bring them, too."

Maria still shook her head. "David's missing his mom a little. That's Linda, my older sister—she stayed in Phoenix to run our restaurant. I wouldn't want him to feel excluded."

"I guess he could come, too."

Maria hesitated. "No, thank you, really, but I wouldn't like to leave—"

"Veronica and the baby? Your mother?" he guessed impatiently. "Hell, let them *all* eat over here. It's silly for you to have to fix two suppers every night."

"But you were only supposed to provide room and board for me. Feeding my whole family wasn't part of the deal. We planned on buying our own groceries."

"So I'll take something out of your pay," Ben said with growing exasperation. Could the woman never do as she was asked? "Will that make you feel better."

A plastic cup, jiggling in time to the bass beat, walked itself off the edge of the counter and fell to the floor. They watched it roll to a stop next to the refrigerator. He saw a look close to pity on her face. "All right. It *will* be more convenient to just cook one meal. If you're sure the extra noise won't bother you?"

The sound of the TV in the living room added itself to the music. "You're kidding, right?" Ben said with a wry smile.

"You ready to go, boss?" Harvey stood at the door, peering through the open screen. He grimaced at the sound that assaulted his ears. "You having a party or something?"

"Connor" was Ben's succinct reply as he picked up his dusty hat from the table and jammed it low on his forehead.

Harvey nodded, understanding. "Howdy there, Maria. I see you're still here. The boss told me—"

"Shut up, Harvey," Ben said, pushing him aside to go through the door.

"Hi, Harvey. I was expecting you for lunch."

"I have my own place about ten miles down the road. You probably passed it on your way here. I take my meals there."

"I see."

"I like my independence," Harvey told her.

"And Vergie won't let him step foot inside her kitchen," Ben added as he started down the steps.

"That's true. She's a mean-spirited woman. Of course, she's always had a crush on me, you know." Harvey gave Maria a wink before following Ben.

"She can't stand the sight of you," Ben corrected.

"It's those squinty little pig eyes of hers, distorting her view, that's what it is."

"Shut up, Harvey."

Maria stood at the door and watched the two men walk away, smiling as she listened to their nonstop bickering. She saw Ben pause at the garden and strained to hear what he was saying.

"I've never seen this old garden look so good, have you, Harvey? I think you ladies—and gentleman—deserve a break, don't you, Harvey?"

Maria saw all heads look up expectantly.

"I bet a swim would sure feel good right about now. Why don't you kids call it a day here and go for a swim down in the pond?" The children began to clamor with excitement. Ben turned and respectfully addressed their grandmother who rocked under a tree. "The water's only three-foot deep in the middle so it's safe for them, if it would be all right with you?"

The woman regally inclined her head, giving her seal of approval.

"Get going, then." Ben made shooing motions with his hands. Maria saw he had a satisfied smile on his face as he watched them scamper out of the garden, unmindful of where their feet landed or what they squashed, followed more carefully, but just as eagerly, by the two women.

For several minutes, Maria stared into the now-empty garden. What possible problems could Ben have with his son that would force him to put up with a table full of strangers every night to avoid being alone with him? She thought about the man who'd just offered her and her family not only a summer away from the city but also food at his table and recreation on his property.

It was strange to consider a man...as a man. Maria hadn't thought about a man, period, in the five years since her husband, Marcus, had died. But Ben Calder had made her aware of his masculinity within minutes, and had made her aware of herself, too. She'd forgotten what it felt like to have her stomach muscles tighten when she met a man's eyes; she'd forgotten the way her skin could tingle when she stood close to a man. It felt strange to notice the hair on a man's arms, the strength of his fingers as he'd twisted that jar lid, to notice the beginning of whiskers on a strong chin. Strange, not exactly unpleasant, but it had just been so long. So long.

Maria gave herself a mental shake. Enough! Ben Calder was a man, all right, and men were to be given a wide berth. Maria had learned her lesson about men as a child, learned it the hard way, when her father had walked out the door on her ninth birthday. Maria still remembered the look on her father's face when her mother had told him she was pregnant again, pregnant with Veronica. His face had gone as white as the frosting on her cake, and even the glow of the candles couldn't add warmth to the hunted look that came into his eyes. He'd sang "Happy Birthday" to her, he'd watched her open her presents, he'd kissed her and tucked her into bed, and then, sometime during the night, while she'd slept with her new birthday doll tucked under her arm, he'd left.

That's what men did. They left. When the going got tough, they left. They left the women—and the children.

Her late husband had been different. Maria had made sure of that before she married him. Marcus Soldata had been a good man, a solid man, and if Maria had occasionally longed for a passion it was not in her husband's nature to give, she stoically suppressed such longings. She had not married Marcus for passion. She'd married him because he would always be there. He had loved her and he had loved his daughters in a quiet, comforting way. Marcus Soldata would have never left his family and, indeed, it took a fiery car crash to take him away from them.

But Marcus appeared to be an exception to the men in her family, Maria thought wryly. Not only had her father found family life too much for him, but last year her brother-in-law had run off with his secretary, leaving her older sister, Linda, to raise David with little help or interest from him. The women had drawn their protective circle tight around the bitter Linda and bewildered little boy, and the restaurant had managed to keep food on their table—barely. Then

when Veronica's husband's phone calls and letters had
abruptly stopped coming from Tucson, well...Maria hadn'
been too surprised.

Benjamin Calder was just a man, Maria told hersel
sternly, starting out to the garden to finish the weeding. An
she had best remember it.

The children were in high spirits at the supper table, fresh
from their swim, and Maria tried to hush them as she be
gan to pass the food. She cast a worried glance at Ben, bu
he didn't seem to mind the noise. In fact, the only time a
frown came to his face was when he looked Connor's way.

Connor had disappeared into his room after his arrival
not to be seen again until he was called for supper. Now he
sat at the table between his father and Veronica, the head
phones of a portable CD player plugging his ears, nodding
his head to a beat inaudible to the rest of them.

"Connor, could you take those off, please?" The polite
tone was obviously a struggle for Ben. Connor's head con
tinued to bob. He tapped his fork against his plate, keeping
time to his own private drummer as he waited for a dish o.
garlic bread to make its way to him.

"Connor!"

Connor helped himself to four pieces of bread.

Striking like a snake, Ben snatched the headphones from
his son's head. "I asked you to take these off. I don't wan
to see them at the dinner table again."

"Hey!" Connor pulled the thin piece of metal out of his
father's grip, cradling it protectively in his lap. "Mom always let's me."

"I'm sure she does" was Ben's sardonic reply.

Connor shot his father a sullen look before reaching for
the heavy platter of spaghetti Trisha struggled to pass to
him, ladling a mound onto his plate without a word.

"A thank-you to Trisha would be appropriate, don't you think?"

Ben's request was an order and Connor gave a loud, persecuted sigh. "Dad, lighten up, will ya? You're such a hard ass."

"Watch your mouth. You know damned well I don't allow you to use that kind of language."

"Yeah, right. So you're going to send me to bed without any supper?" The toss of bangs made the question a clear challenge.

Ben's voice was icy. "That can be arranged."

Maria watched father and son stare at each other, testing, identical gray eyes probing just how far each was willing to go this time. She glanced uneasily at the children, dismayed to find them watching the exchange with wide-eyed interest.

Connor was the first to look away. He straightened from his slouch and turned to the little girl. "Thank you very much." Then he addressed Maria. "Mrs. Soldata, this spaghetti smells absolutely delicious. It's one of my favorite meals. And I'm looking forward to some authentic Mexican food while I'm here. I'm especially fond of chicken enchiladas. Dad, would you care for some spaghetti?" He held the platter toward his father, smiling agreeably.

Maria couldn't help herself. She laughed out loud. What a rogue! Connor's smile became impish and, as he'd obviously planned, his father's face relaxed and there even appeared a ghost of a rueful smile on it. From then on, Connor was absolutely charming, and Maria became more and more amused as she watched the skillful con artist wind everyone around his finger. Even Veronica, jaded as she'd become lately, was soon smiling and blushing at the boy's outrageous flattery. And when he complimented their

mother on her dress, the old woman had to struggle to keep
her disapproving frown.

"I mean it, Mrs. Romero, that shade of brown is very attractive on you. A mature woman such as yourself should
always wear classic colors."

Ben listened to the baloney his son was dishing out and
the way the women smiled indulgently at him and could only
shake his head. Connor had always handled his mother in
exactly the same way. Lori let him get away with murder and
his stepfather blatantly bribed him to keep him out of his
hair. The end result was a spoiled, willful, soon-to-be-man
with a strong aversion to hard work. And Ben was at a loss
as to how to change any of it.

"Come on, Veronica," Connor was saying. "Let's drive
into Wyberg and see what they do for excitement out here
in the boonies."

"No thanks, Connor. Not tonight."

"Come on," he wheedled. "There's no cable out here,
you know. I'm going to go nuts without MTV."

"I can't. Ashley will wake up from her nap soon and I'll
have to bath her and feed her again."

"Aw, let Maria take care of her own kids. You've done
your baby-sitting thing for the day."

The women glanced swiftly at each other. Ben was surprised when none of them volunteered to correct Connor's
mistaken assumption that the baby was Maria's.

Veronica just shook her head.

The petulant look returned to Connor's face in a flash.
"Fine!" he snapped. He scraped his chair from the table.
"But I'm not going to sit here and rot."

With a flip of bangs and an insolent, "Later," he
slammed out the door. The roar of an engine and spurting
gravel said his more eloquent goodbyes.

The room was uncomfortably silent, the adults making a studied effort to avoid each other's eyes. A cry from the infant seat in the corner was a welcome diversion.

"Right on schedule," Veronica said with false brightness. She picked up the crying baby, murmuring soft, comforting sounds.

"Kids, why don't you clear the table?" Maria said in the same too-cheerful manner. "Trisha, make sure you rinse those plates before you put them in the dishwasher, okay?"

"Yes, Mama." The children hopped from their chairs and began stacking plates and carrying them to the kitchen. Soon rattling dishes, running water and childish arguing could be heard coming from the next room.

Just an obedient "Yes, Mama," and three children went to work? Ben thought in amazement. No whining. No back talk. He couldn't remember the last time Connor had responded to the simplest request without some smart comment.

He put his elbows on the table and cleared his throat. "Uh, sorry about Connor. He's been having a rough time of it since his mother and I divorced."

The women nodded sympathetically. "It can be hard on kids. David's still reeling from my sister's divorce," Maria told him. "I hope he manages to adjust pretty soon. How long ago was your divorce?"

"Six years."

When Maria looked surprised, Ben realized what he'd said. "I guess six years is a long time to adjust. Maybe I can't blame all of Connor's behavior on the divorce. I mean, your girls seemed to be doing okay."

"I'm a widow, though. Maybe that makes a difference."

Ben was surprised; he'd assumed she was divorced. "I'm sorry."

"It was a family tragedy," Mrs. Romero's voice unexpectedly crackled out. "Marcus was the only man in the whole bunch worth a *centavo*."

"He was a good father," Veronica agreed, patting Ashley with a wistful look.

"A good husband." Mrs. Romero nodded.

"For our family, he was a saint," Veronica said.

"He had that one problem, though." The old woman looked very wise.

"What's that, Mama?"

"He died."

The three women's eyes met. Maria's lips were the first to twitch. Suddenly, they were all laughing. Rich, full laughter, laughter of shared tears and understood fears, the laughter of the women who were left, who held the family together, who made due, got by—who survived.

And Ben felt as excluded as if he were watching from the other side of a glass wall.

Ben padded in stocking feet into the kitchen and ran a glass of water from the faucet. He'd been working in the office, going over the accounts, but was finding it difficult to concentrate. The sounds of soft, feminine voices, accented by the higher notes of the children, coming through the open windows of the study had made him restless. Once again he found himself staring out the kitchen window, surreptitiously watching Maria and her family enjoy the evening from the porch of the guest house.

He strained his ears, trying to make out individual words, but he couldn't. It was only rhythm, rising and falling, carried to him and past him on the cooling breeze, engulfing him and caressing him but never allowing him to be a part of it.

He managed to pick out Maria's form where she sat on the steps surrounded by the children. Her long hair hung around her shoulders and seemed to flow and merge with the shadows, making her appear ethereal and without substance. But Ben knew how far that was from the truth. Maria was turning out to be the most real, solid and determined woman he'd ever met.

What kind of life must she have back in Phoenix that would force her to stay in a place where she'd been clearly ordered to leave? he wondered. What kind of desperation must she have felt to disobey him, knowing she faced an embarrassing scene when he returned?

Maria's voice, lifted in a Spanish lullaby, came to him, the words incomprehensibly foreign and yet universally understood. Ben felt a protective surge of emotion well up from somewhere deep inside of him. He didn't want her to have to fight so hard, to have to courageously face the enemy, even if the enemy was only himself. He wanted... He wanted...

Ben set down the glass and moved away from the window, away from the disturbing sound of her voice. As he made his way back to his office, he heard only silence, the loudest, loneliest silence of all—the silence of a parent waiting in the night for a teenager to return.

Chapter Three

"One... Are you ready? Two... Hold your breath." Ten toes curled into Ben's shoulders as he gripped Tina's thin legs, steadying her above him. "Three!" He launched her up and over his head, smiling as she splashed into the pond and came up wet and sputtering, dark hair dripping into her eyes, demanding to do it again.

"No! It's my turn!" Trisha shouted, jumping up and down next to him.

"Stop that, you're soaking me." Maria laughed. She stood beside Ben, thigh-deep in the pond. The bottom of her blue shorts were wet, darkened almost to black, and her white flowered tank top was splashed with muddy pond water.

"This is the last one," Ben warned the children as he lifted Trisha onto his shoulders. "You're wearing me out. And watch my hat this time." With a flick of his powerful arms, he flipped the girl into the water next to her sister and cousin, using one hand to clamp his cowboy hat to his head.

Dressed only in ragged cutoff jeans and ever-present hat, Ben squinted into the late-afternoon sun, watching for her small head to bob to the surface. Satisfied, he turned to Maria with a whoop. "You're next!"

Maria's squeal was loud and unladylike as she ran for the edge of the pond, its muddy bottom sucking at her feet. She made the grassy bank and darted for the safety of the quilt they'd left spread on the ground next to the cedar fence that separated the pond from the horse pasture. Ben was only a step or two behind her as she collapsed onto the blanket. Laughing, trying to catch her breath, she tossed her hair over her shoulders and threw her head back to look up at him, supporting herself on her arms.

Ben let the sun warm his bare back while he appreciated the sight she presented. Maria's hair was free from the braid she usually wore and reddish highlights shot through the dark chocolate mass. Her wet top clung to the swell of her stomach, emphasizing full breasts that raised and lowered with each quick breath. Water ran down her long, tanned legs and soaked into the blanket beneath them, and Ben couldn't keep his eyes from tracing one particular drop that trickled along the curve of her calf and wrapped itself around a slender ankle.

Maria patted the blanket next to her. "Have a seat."

Swallowing with a suddenly dry mouth, Ben lowered himself onto the worn quilt. He pushed his hat down over his eyes, ostensibly to ward off the setting sun but also to hide the uncomfortable turn his thoughts had taken.

"Thanks again for letting the kids use the pond," Maria said. "They've been in it every afternoon this week."

"I'm glad it's getting some use. Connor's sort of out-grown it, I guess. He used to practically live down here. If he wasn't in it, he was next to it, catching frogs or grass-hoppers or waterskippers."

"David already has a jar full of those horrible things."
Maria made a face. "They look like spiders to me."

"The girls don't seem to mind them." Ben watched the
three children who now squatted among the cattails near the
edge of the water, trying to guide the leggy insects into
David's half-submerged mayonnaise jar.

"They're a couple of tomboys, all right. Which is sort of
surprising when you consider their father died when they
were so young. Not much male influence in their lives."

"How long ago did he die?"

"Five years," Maria answered matter-of-factly. She
rubbed her feet back and forth on the grass to try to wipe off
some of the mud that covered their soles.

"They probably don't remember him, then?"

Maria shook her head and Ben found himself suddenly
curious. She certainly didn't sound like she still grieved the
loss of her husband.

"What happened?" he ventured, willing to probe a little.

"Car crash."

"That's too bad."

"Hmm." Maria nodded.

Ben turned his head to look at her from under the brim of
his hat, trying to gauge her reaction to his questions. But she
didn't appear uncomfortable; in fact, she had a slight smile
on her face as she watched the children begin a rowdy sword
fight with broken-off cattails. "Did he work in your family's restaurant, too?"

"No, he was an auto mechanic." This time she volunteered more information. "He had his own shop. Marcus
was a very good mechanic. A lousy businessman, but a good
mechanic." She spoke with wry affection. "He gave credit
to every relative we had, and between the two of us, that's

most of south Phoenix. He was always helping some high school kid fix up his car for free."

"He sounds like a good man. Your mother and Veronica spoke highly of him the other night."

"They loved Marcus."

Ben was surprised to find himself wondering if Maria had loved Marcus. "Tough for the girls, being so little when he died."

"He was a wonderful father. Kind. Dependable. A good man."

The gentleness in her voice had Ben shifting uncomfortably on the soft blanket. *A wonderful father.* No one could accuse him of that these days.

"Stop that, Trisha," Maria called. "You're going to put somebody's eye out." She jumped to her feet and started down toward the pond.

Ben watched her snap off the sharp, pointed ends of the heavy brown stalks before returning them to the children. Then, without warning, she broke off a stalk for herself and pointed it at David's stomach. *"En garde,"* she challenged. The fight was on—shouting, splashing, tumbling children, with Maria right in the middle.

Ben remembered playing the same game with Connor years ago, and the memory brought a curve to his lips. It was good to hear childish laughter on the ranch again. Maria and her family had been there almost a week, and Ben was surprised at how much he was enjoying the children. Noisy meals, full of spilled milk and breathless chatter; tracked mud on the hardwood floors and smudged fingerprints on the refrigerator; shouts and giggles piercing the normally subdued, blue-gray evening sounds. And dark, excited eyes always smiling at him, happy to tell him about their day, eager and pleased to have his attention.

Ben's smile faded.

Connor had looked at him like that, a long time ago. Then, bit by bewildering bit, Connor's gray, loving eyes had turned sullen. They'd begun to skitter away when he'd try to hold them, until eventually they wouldn't raise to meet his at all. And if they ever did, Ben would almost wish they hadn't, because they would be filled with antagonism, resentment—dark emotions Ben didn't even want to name. He didn't think he could bear to watch it happen again with another child.

With determined movements, Ben pulled on socks and his dusty cowboy boots and started back toward the house without a word of farewell. Those long, dark legs that had tempted him all week came with two little girls attached, he reminded himself sternly. It was a package deal and he wasn't going to touch it with a ten-foot pole.

"So where's Connor?" Maria asked, picking out a pair of David's dirt-encrusted jeans from the pile of clothes heaped on the floor and stuffing them into the sink.

"How should I know?" Veronica responded innocently.

"Yeah, right. Like he hasn't been following you around like a lovesick puppy." Maria added a splash of detergent to the jeans and turned on the faucet. "How much longer are you going to be able to keep from going to Wyberg with him? He asks every single night."

"Hey! *Chaquita!* Let's rock 'n' roll!" Mrs. Romero's imitation of Connor, in her heavily accented English, caused all three women to sputter with laughter as they did the family's laundry in the kitchen sink of the guest house.

"So how's it feel to be the 'older woman'?" Maria teased.

"You're a great one to talk, big sister!" Veronica said huffily. "You think we haven't noticed you and the boss making goo-goo eyes at each other?"

"We are not!"

PATTI STANDARD 49

"Oh, really? Let's see—" Veronica pretended to think. "He tells you to go but then let's you stay. You're on a first name basis in less than twenty-four hours. He thinks you're the best cook to ever turn on a stove. He joins us on the porch last night and doesn't even notice when the rest of us go in to bed—we don't hear you come in for two more hours. You're right, of course. No goo-goo eyes. What could I be thinking of?"

Maria felt warmth creep up her face. She'd been half expecting some comment from her sister after spending so long alone with Ben last night. Her telltale flush was sure to make it seem like something it wasn't. They'd done no more than talk. And if two hours had sped by, if she'd found him fascinating and incredibly sexy and intelligent and amusing, if she'd had to continually remind herself that she wasn't the least bit interested in any man in spite of the way he made her toes curl—well, that was nothing she had to tell her sister.

"Ben's just being friendly," Maria insisted, willing the heat from her cheeks.

"And so's Connor! Besides, he really is sort of cute." Veronica swished a handful of baby clothes in the rinse water. "Connor, I mean. Ben's a hunk, too, but Connor's really cute for somebody as young as he is."

"He's darling," Maria agreed. "And he can act quite mature for his age—when he's not around his father, that is."

The women nodded their heads, considering for a moment the obviously sorry state of affairs between father and son.

"What that boy needs is a whippin'," their mother pronounced. "And from the look on Señor Calder's face when he starts his smart-mouth talk, he's going to get it one of these days."

All heads nodded again. "One day, I tell you, I'm going to take my scissors and—" Mrs. Romero held up a wet hand and made a scissor-cutting motion with two of her fingers. "Snip, snip, snip! No more bangs to go flip, flop, toss!" Her lined brown face transformed itself into a parody of Connor's indolent expression and she twitched her head with its neat gray bun as if to throw back a length of offending hair.

Maria and Veronica began to giggle and they laughed until they had to lean against the sink for support. Even Ashley, from her infant carrier on the floor next to their feet, took her little fist from her mouth long enough to squeal once or twice, joining in the merriment.

Veronica smiled at her daughter and reached down to adjust the swinging toys that hung from the carrier so they dangled within Ashley's reach. Then her expression turned serious. "I know you've both been waiting for me to say something to Connor."

"It's your decision," Maria said, scrubbing at a stain on the knee of a pair of jeans.

"He just sort of assumed that Ashley was yours, and now it seems kind of awkward to bring up the subject."

Maria nodded. They worked silently, washing, rinsing, wringing, then dropping the wet clothes into a basket to be hung on the line. Veronica was quiet but she obviously continued to struggle with the matter. Her movements became more and more agitated. Finally, she threw a shirt into the rinse water with enough force it splashed water across the front of her blouse and onto the floor.

"I got a baby food grinder for my birthday!" she burst out. "I haven't slept through the night in six months." She grabbed the wet shirt and plunged it up and down. "I—" Plunge. "Have—" Plunge. *"Stretch marks!"* She glared at her family defiantly. "It's nice to pretend just for once, just for a little while— He thinks I'm pretty. I know he's just a kid but—Roberto still hasn't called!'' She dissolved into tears.

Maria gathered her weeping sister into her arms, rocking and soothing her. Her wet hands patted her back while she sobbed and they stood together in the puddle on the floor. ''I know, sweetie. I know,'' she whispered over and over.

What harm would it do for them to act as if Veronica were only Ashley's aunt? Maria asked herself. Just for the short time Connor was here? Her ego was fragile to the point of shattering since her husband had been gone. A little male attention, even from a seventeen-year-old with an overdose of hormones, couldn't do any harm.

''Mama,'' Maria said, ''I don't see any problem with not rushing out and telling Connor he's made a mistake, do you? I mean, it probably won't even come up again. We can watch Ashley in the evenings if Veronica wants to take that trip into Wyberg every now and then, can't we?''

''That's what families are for,'' Mrs. Romero said, stoically continuing with her work.

''And Connor knows I'm married.'' Veronica sniffed. ''Really, he's just being friendly. He's bored, that's all.''

''He's got a harmless little crush and there's nothing wrong with that,'' Maria said firmly.

Veronica gave them a weepy smile and by the time a knock sounded on the door a few minutes later they were chattering and smiling once again, the floor mopped dry.

''Hi, Ben, come on in,'' Maria called.

''Hi.'' Ben took off his hat as he entered the kitchen. ''So what are you hardworking women up to this afternoon?''

''Laundry.''

''Ah.'' He nodded and glanced briefly at the piles of clothes on the floor.

''Is there something you wanted me to do?'' Maria asked.

"Nope. You're supposed to take the afternoons off since you have to work evenings, remember? I just wanted to let you know I invited Harvey for supper tonight. Is that okay?"

"Well, of course it's all right. You can invite whoever you want to your own table."

"Harvey wants to take advantage of Vergie being gone. He says she gives him indigestion. I'm never sure if he means her cooking or her personality."

Maria laughed and gathered up another handful of clothes to add to the sink.

Ben frowned as he watched her. "What are you doing?"

"I told you. Laundry."

"By hand? All of it!"

Maria nodded, puzzled by his obvious displeasure.

"For God's sake, I have a washer and dryer."

"Well, I don't."

"So you're going to wash laundry for six people and a *baby* by hand rather than use my washing machine?"

"Ashley wears disposable diapers. It's not that big of a deal."

Ben strode up behind her and thrust his hand into the sink, pulling the plug. "Take all this stuff into the house and put it into the washing machine," he ordered. "And then put it into the dryer. And then repeat that process as many times as you need to, as often as you need to, from now on. Is that clear!"

Maria meekly nodded her head, speechless.

"Well, all right, then." Ben backed away, obviously uncomfortable now at his outburst. "That's settled, then."

"Thank you," Maria said.

"Yeah, thanks," Veronica echoed.

Ben's eye was caught by the basket of wet clothes sitting on the table and he paused. His look of irritation disap-

eared, replaced by a sly smile. He reached out and, with his
ttle finger, caught up a scrap of cloth. He dangled a pair
f red satin panties with their lacy trim and tiny bows in
ront of the women. "I can see how something like this
might need to be hand washed, though."

"Ben!" Maria snatched her panties away from him and
acked them at the bottom of the basket, her face as red as
ae wisp of cloth she was hiding. "Those are Mama's, you
now."

Ben and Veronica burst out laughing.

"You laugh!" Mrs. Romero pretended outrage. "What?
ou do not think I'm a 'hot tamale'?"

"Of course I do, Señora Romero." Ben gave her an ex-
ggerated wink. "The hottest."

"Hah! Don't you have work to do? I hear a cow calling
ou." She pushed him toward the door, prodding him with
er walking stick, barely giving him time to jam his hat back
n his head.

Still smiling, the women began to gather up the remain-
ag clothes to take into the house to the washing machine.

"That Ben Calder," Mrs. Romero said, shaking her head.
¿Que hombre, no?"

"Sí," Maria replied. What a man.

Ben was pleased to hear the washing machine still chug-
ing when he came down the stairs after his shower that
vening. He looked into the utility room and felt a sense of
atisfaction to see the small shirts and miniature shorts
eatly folded and stacked next to his and Connor's clothes
n the folding table. Doing laundry by hand, for God's
ake, he thought, disgruntled once again. Why didn't she
ust ask to use his washing machine? He didn't know why
er strength and independence annoyed him so much, but
 did.

He heard laughter coming from the kitchen, a norma
sound these days. When he passed through the doorway h
saw Maria piling plates onto Harvey's waiting arms while h
faded eyes twinkled down at her and she sassed back at hin
And, in that instance, Ben realized why it bothered him tha
Maria was so self-sufficient. Ben Calder was a provider, lik
his father before him. He took care of his ranch, his live
stock, his land and the people on it. He should be takin
care of her, too. Not because of any special attraction h
might feel for her, he told himself, but because it was a pa
of what he did—who he was. Yet Maria didn't seem to hav
any use for him at all.

She didn't seem to have any use for men in general. Nor
of the women did. Although they tended to watch the
words in front of the children, even Connor had noticed i
now that he'd been forced to take off his headphones lon
enough to join in mealtime conversations.

"Did you hear what she said?" Connor was saying t
David as they all sat down at the table. Veronica had re
sponded to one of his latest attempts at wooing with th
sniffed put-down, "typical male." He pointed his fork at th
little boy. "You women are going to give this guy a con
plex. He's surrounded by females. It's not natural. What d
you have against men, anyway?"

"We don't have anything against men," Maria said as sh
reached for a roll. "Men are great."

"But?" Ben prompted, sensing an unspoken qualifica
tion.

"But nothing. It's just that men—" She hesitated, car
fully buttering the roll. "They need a lot of attention," sh
finished diplomatically.

Her mother gave a snort of agreement. "A *lot* of atter
tion. You're better off with a pet."

"Like a cat?" Trisha asked.

"*Sí, un gato.* A cat is much cleaner."

"And a dog is more loyal," Veronica asserted positively.

"You can't just leave them on a table to play by themselves like a hamster," Trisha said.

"Or my goldfish," Tina chimed in, as serious as only a six-year-old can be.

Harvey was guffawing loudly by now. "You women been around them city men too long," he declared. "What you need is a last-of-a-dying-breed type. Like Ben here."

"Shut up, Harvey," Ben said.

"It's true!" Harvey insisted. "It said so right in our own Wyberg newspaper. Ben Calder, Last Of A Dying Breed—right on the front page in big ol' letters."

"Shut up, Harvey," all of the children chanted in unison, catching Ben as he started to open his mouth.

Harvey smirked at his employer. "Yup, a whole page about Calder Ranch and Ben, the way he took over when his daddy died and made it one of the money-makingest small ranches in the state. It flat out said he was the best catch in all of northern Arizona. Right there in black-and-white."

Maria loved the way a slow flush crept up Ben's neck. "I've got to hear more about this," she teased. "The best catch in northern Arizona?"

"It's true." Harvey nodded. "Why, take MaryBeth Parker—"

"Shut—" Ben caught himself just in time.

"What about MaryBeth Parker?" Maria asked, watching the red make its way up to Ben's cheekbones.

"She swooned."

"She had the flu," Ben insisted.

"Nope. She swooned. You asked her to that dance over at Flagstaff and she fell right down at your feet in the middle of Waddell's Market. There's witnesses, boss! Don't try to deny it."

"Harvey, she had a stomach flu. She was in bed for a week after that."

"Only a week? I can name a dozen women in these parts who've taken a lot longer than a week to get over you, boss. There's Stella McClaskey over at the feed store. She's been trying to get in your pants for fifteen years—"

"Shut up, Harvey." This time every adult at the table joined in the admonishment. Harvey looked guiltily around at the listening children. "Well, it's true," he insisted. "Last of a dying breed, that's what he is and the women know it. Course I am, too," he said with wagging eyebrows and a comical leer. "Just ask Vergie. I know, I know. Shut up, Harvey."

Another fight. Ben sighed and pushed away the papers in front of him. He switched off the desk light and rubbed at the bridge of his nose. Once again, Connor had refused to ride out with Ben and Harvey that morning to help with the chores. Too busy, he said. But as far as Ben could see, the only thing Connor was busy doing was watching videos. Ben didn't know what else he did, shut in his room by himself all day. He was almost human at dinner and in the evenings— trying to impress Veronica, no doubt. But he never lifted a finger to help after the meal, just flopped back in front of the TV.

This evening had been no different. As soon as Maria and her family had left, Connor had done his Jekyll-and-Hyde number once again, his handsome face taking on the bored and petulant expression he seemed to reserve for his father alone.

"Thought you might like a game of poker," Ben had said, flipping through a deck of cards. "You were pretty good last time you were up here."

"I was just a kid then. You let me win." Connor hadn't even bothered to look away from the television.

"Bet I won't have to this time."

"No, thanks."

"Come on. We haven't had a chance to talk since you got up here."

"Don't try to pretend you give a damn, Dad!" Connor had exploded. "I don't want to play any stupid card game. Why don't you just leave me alone!" Then he'd run up the stairs to shut himself in his room again.

Ben's shoulders slumped as he sat in the darkened office. No matter what he said, it was always the wrong thing. Almost without thinking, Ben found himself on his way outside to the guest house, unable to stand another moment in the house, knowing Connor sulked upstairs behind a closed door. He had no idea whether the right thing to do was go to him or stay away from him. So, just as he had last night, Ben avoided the whole problem by leaving—by leaving his family and going to hers, in spite of the vow he'd made to keep his distance.

It was late and the children were already in bed, but the women were still on the porch, each with a needle and thread in hand and a piece of clothing to be mended on their laps.

Maria heard the door slam and watched Ben walk across the lawn toward her. Automatically, she moved over to make room for him on the step beside her.

"Hi," he said, lowering himself, stretching out his long legs.

The women switched smoothly from the Spanish they'd been using among themselves. "Good evening, Señor Ben," Mrs. Romero greeted him.

"Good evening, *señora*. I hope you're not straining your eyes in this dim light."

"My eyes were strained long ago. A few more loose buttons won't make them much worse."

"Well, I'm tired of stabbing myself by moonlight," Veronica proclaimed. She hopped off the porch swing. "I'm heading for bed. Ashley'll be up just about the time I close my eyes. Coming, Mama?"

Her mother heaved herself up from the rocking chair, gathering her sewing in one hand and her stick in the other. Good-nights passed among them and no one questioned that Maria would stay outside with Ben.

They sat in companionable silence for a while, as comfortable together as they had been last night. Maria had been so surprised when he'd shown up, looking almost wistful as he'd asked if he could join them. Since that afternoon at the pond when he'd left so abruptly, he'd seemed to avoid the children as much as possible, and Maria had worried they were getting on his nerves. But last night he'd wrestled with David and teased the girls and flattered the women until even her mother had relaxed her usually forbidding countenance enough to smile once or twice at him. And after everyone else had gone to bed, they'd sat talking in the dark for a long, long time.

Maria could feel the tension that Ben had brought with him tonight slowly, visibly, draining away.

"Connor?" she asked.

A curt nod. "Better not to talk about it."

Maria said nothing more, just waited while the quiet outside helped to quiet him inside. The mountains on the horizon were outlined by an almost imperceptible blanching of the midnight blue sky, the only proof that the sun had recently passed that way. A rustle in the lilac bush next to the house marked the movements of something small and nervous, hurrying to safety. Moths circled the covered bulb that lit the porch, courageously battling the light, offering their bodies in sacrifice.

One large brown moth swooped low and Maria flicked her head to ward it off, tangling its wings in the heavy mass of her pony tail. Instinctively, she reached up to dislodge it, but her swiping movements only entangled the moth further. Ben caught her hand, stopping her futile efforts, and with his free hand he carefully plucked the creature from its silky net and let it flutter off.

"Thanks," Maria started to say, but her words caught as she saw the way Ben looked at the hand he still held cradled in his. He seemed fascinated, and slowly, with intense concentration, he passed a thumb over her roughened skin, skimming the calluses on her palm. Self-conscious, Maria tried to pull away.

"Don't," she told him, embarrassed by what his touch would discover. "My hands are a mess."

But he didn't release her; instead, he pushed her fingers open, uncurling them until her hand lay motionless in his. "You work," he said, a simple statement. With one finger he slowly touched the thickened skin at the base of each of her fingers. Maria shivered at the intimacy of the caress, bothered that such a simple touch could start such a trembling within her.

She cleared her throat, trying to sound normal, as if the tremble in her hand was of no consequence. "I used to wear rubber gloves but every time you leave the kitchen to serve a customer you have to take them off. It was too much trouble." She swallowed, the trembling worsening. Unable to stand it any longer, she snatched her hand away and tucked it between her knees.

"Tell me about your restaurant," Ben said, letting her go.

"Casa Juanita?" Maria smiled, willing herself to relax. "We make the best chicken tacos in Phoenix."

"It's named for your mother, I take it?"

"Mama started the business after— Well, she started it when I was nine. She'd take us girls with her in the evenings—the restaurant's only open for supper—and we'd watch Veronica while Mama cooked. We sort of grew up with the restaurant, working after school and during the summer until eventually we took over most of the business when Mama's arthritis got too bad.

An unconscious frown creased her forehead. "It was good for a part-time job when we were all married, but since my husband died, and now that Linda's divorced—that's David's mother—we're trying to support three families on the one business." Maria shrugged. "It's been—"

"Hard," Ben finished for her.

She shrugged again. "We're getting by."

"How can you all take off for the summer?" Ben asked.

Maria's laugh was short and hard. "The problem isn't our taking off, the problem is all our customers taking off. We're right next door to the university, so when school's out we lose our customer base. We're not big enough or fancy enough or located in the right place to get much of the tourist business. Linda can handle the place alone for the summer, and God knows she needs the money. We all usually get second jobs in the summer, anyway, to tide us over. Things will be better when I graduate in December. That will really help."

"Graduate?" Ben sounded surprised.

Maria nodded. "I've been going to night school forever. It's only a two-year degree in accounting, but it's a step in the right direction. The restaurant can't support all of us for much longer now that the kids are getting older and more expensive." Her voice took on a startling fierceness. "And I don't want my girls to end up cleaning somebody else's dirty dishes their whole life."

Ben was moved by that fierceness. He had never had to worry about what he would do with his life. Calder Ranch was in his blood just like generations before him. The thought of leaving Calder Ranch had never occurred to him; he'd always known he would take it over when his father died. And though there had been occasional lean years, he'd always felt secure about his future and about Connor's. Connor might not show much interest in the ranch now, but he was still young.

Once again Ben felt that protective surge. He felt her slender body ever so lightly brush against his arm—so small and delicate and carrying the everyday scents of garlic from cooking his supper and soap from cleaning his home.

Gently, he reached out to touch her cheek and turned her face toward him. He told himself to stop, to let her go, to not allow himself to feel even a hint of the smoothness of her skin. Her eyes, larger and darker than ever, all hollows and shadows in the moonlight, gazed at him, startled and hesitant.

Slowly, ignoring his inner warning, Ben lowered his head, fascinated by the way her lips parted in spite of their trembling, as if anticipating and fearing his kiss at the same time. He heard her catch her breath and felt the softness of her breast against his arm as she leaned toward him.

"Waa-aahh!" The breathless stillness that enveloped them was shattered by the baby's cry. Maria jerked back as if burned and scrambled to her feet with almost guilty haste. "I—I'd better go help Veronica with the baby." She stared at him with huge eyes for a moment, a picture of indecision, then she turned and disappeared into the darkened house without a backward look.

Ben dropped Harvey off at his tin-roofed house. He maneuvered past the yard full of rusting mattress springs, the scraps of iron from unidentifiable sources, the half a dozen ravaged truck bodies squatting on wooden blocks, the frantically barking dingos who raced him to the mailbox, and drove the rest of the way home in weary silence. Since Connor had arrived he hadn't been able to bear the sound of the truck radio anymore, even tuned to the mellow country western music he listened to. It had been a physically exhausting day mending fence. His hands ached from the repeated stabs of the sharp barbs on the wire that penetrated his thick leather gloves as if they were butter. All he wanted was a shower, supper and, in spite of the still-early hour, bed.

A smile touched the edges of his dry, sun-chapped lips. He mentally revised his list to include an hour or so on the porch with Maria. It had become a nightly ritual and something he looked forward to all day.

Their almost-kiss had never been repeated and, by unspoken agreement, they kept a good foot between them on the steps every night. Maria had determinedly tried to lump him back in with Harvey and Connor as just one of "the men" to be treated in that irritating way she had—as if men were minor annoyances who always seemed to be in the way of the hardworking, long-suffering women. But Ben saw the way her eyes strayed to him at the supper table and the way she subtly stiffened with awareness when he entered the room. There were some sparks jumping between them—Ben knew it, and the more he told himself to stand back, the closer he found himself inching toward the flame. Dammit, he was playing with fire and didn't seem to be able to make himself stop until he had third-degree burns.

It was the challenge, he told himself, that kept him going back to her night after night. Harvey had been right when he'd summed up the local women's predatory attitude toward him since his divorce. Maria was so blatantly unimpressed it was almost insulting. That's all it was, Ben repeated, just a challenge. The value of men was something so obvious in the male-oriented life of ranching. It was ludicrous that he should have to defend his sex to some slip of a *señorita*. He'd show her the type of men the northern Arizona sun grew—men who worked hard, laughed harder... and loved hardest of all. After all, he wasn't the last of a dying breed for nothing.

He parked the truck between the green station wagon that hadn't moved since its arrival and the red sports car that disappeared for hours every evening. He stretched his cramped muscles and couldn't help but look around for the children; usually, at least one of them came running to greet him when he got home. When no one appeared, Ben went into the house and started peering into rooms. The kitchen and dining rooms were empty, and he got barely a grunt from Connor who sat in the living room staring at the TV. Then, through the living room window, he saw a flash of color from behind the house. He walked out the kitchen door, past the garden and around the back of the house to the orchard.

All that was visible of Maria was her legs, balanced precariously on an old ladder. From the waist up, she was hidden in the branches and leaves of a cherry tree. Her mother watched the baby who lay on a blanket in the shade, and the three children hung all over the lower branches like monkeys, dropping their cherries into baskets raised up on cardboard boxes on the ground below them.

"Ben!" Little Tina was the first to see him. She swung down from the branch she'd been sitting on and raced to him.

"Whoa, there! Slow down!" He gingerly returned her exuberant hug, holding her at arm's length, trying to avoid the worst of the cherry stains—trying not to compare her greeting with Connor's. The lower half of her face and both her small hands were dyed bright red. "Did you manage to get any in the basket, or did you just eat everything you picked?"

"She ate every single one," her cousin, David, said in disgust, hanging by his knees from a limb. "She's going to puke if she keeps it up." He let his handful of cherries fall like machine gun fire into a waiting basket.

"Am not!"

"Are, too!"

"That's enough, you two." Maria pushed aside a cherry-laden branch to look down at them. "David, I said 'gently.' If you keep dropping them like that we're going to have nothing but cherry juice."

"Sorry, Aunt Maria." He raised himself upright and went back to picking.

"You're home early," Maria said, carefully making her way down the ladder, a firm grip on the bucket she held in one hand by its wire handle. "I haven't started supper yet. I'll get going on it right now."

"That's all right. No hurry. When Harvey ran out of new stories and started repeating himself I decided it was time to call it a day." He watched while Maria emptied her bucket into an almost full basket. "You know, Harvey usually rounds up a couple of friends to come out and help with the cherries. I didn't expect you to do it all yourself."

"I've got lots of helpers." She smiled at the red-stained children. "Although they're probably eating more than they're picking."

"That's fine by me. But I feel sort of uncomfortable with how much Veronica and the kids help out around here. And your mother, too. Gathering the eggs, doing the garden—I feel like Simon Legree."

Maria laughed. "Good heavens, Ben, what else are they going to do all day? Sit around and watch TV? Here, Mama, let me take Ashley. We'll go start some supper, won't we, sweetie?" She picked up the baby from the blanket, set her snugly on her hip and started for the kitchen. She didn't see the way Ben's cheeks turned a dull red until they almost matched the children's. She couldn't have known that Ben would take her comment to heart, that he would think of Connor immobile in front of the television at that very moment.

Maria was peeling potatoes into the sink, Ashley gumming a soggy cracker in her high chair, when she heard raised voices coming from the living room.

"I said, why aren't you out there helping to pick cherries?" Ben sounded furious.

"Hey, like, I'm on vacation."

"And that means you don't ever get off your butt? That's a vacation?"

"It sure doesn't mean I do your slave labor!" Connor shouted back. "You pay them to sweat like that."

"I don't *pay* them anything! Maria's family is helping because somebody along the way taught them a basic respect for hard work, for doing a job because it needs doing. Your mother and I have obviously failed you."

"You can say that again!"

There was a deadly silence and Maria's hands stilled, suddenly afraid that Connor had gone too far. But then she heard the sound of Ben's boots cross the hall and go up the stairs. He was walking away from the fight, but the clipped angry staccato of his steps was proof what it cost him. Maria sighed, leaned over to give Ashley a kiss on the forehead and began to run the scraper over the skin of the potato again.

Chapter Four

"It's *gracias*," Maria corrected Ben for the dozenth time.

"*Gracias*," Ben repeated obediently.

"Roll your *r*'s. Use your tongue. *G-r-r-r-acias*."

"*Gracias*." Ben's *r*'s rolled like square wheels.

"Listen to me, Ben." Tina, perched on Ben's lap on the grass, reached up and cupped his cheeks between her little hands. She watched his mouth intently while she intoned "*Raul, rojo, Roberto, perro*." Her tongue fluttered like a hummingbird.

"*Raul, rojo, Roberto, perro*," Ben gamely recited, the words incomprehensible with Tina's hands distorting his mouth. By this time, the older children had collapsed to the ground, howling in laughter.

"*Perro*," Tina scolded. "Like this." She darted her fingers inside his mouth and grabbed the end of his tongue, yanking it up and down. "*Per-r-r-o*."

"Tina, honey, stop that!" Maria got up from the porch where she sat next to her mother and scooped the child off

Ben, laughing in delight. "That's not going to help. Ben's going to just have to practice on his own."

"But you can't understand a word he says," Tina complained.

"You can, too. Listen to this. *Buenas dias. ¿Como esta? Muy bien, gracias. Hace mucho calor hoy.*"

"And what does *mucho calor* mean?"

"Ahh, it means—"

"See, he doesn't know! He doesn't know!" Tina danced in circles around Ben.

"I do, too. It means... It means, 'a lot of calories.'"

"It means 'very hot,'" Maria informed him dryly.

"I'll show you hot." Ben reached up and pulled her and the child onto his lap, easily holding their wriggling bodies with one arm. He rained kisses onto Tina, growling like a bear while she squealed.

"Mama's turn! Kiss Mama now!" Tina yelled. She slipped, eel-like, through his arms to kneel next to the adults.

Maria's struggles stopped and her eyes grew enormous as she stared up at the man whose face was inches above hers. Ben didn't hesitate; he leaned over and touched his lips to Maria's. It was a quick, chaste kiss in front of the children, but Maria's eyes closed and her stomach muscles tightened just the same, and she felt heat stir uncomfortably deep inside, burning a path to a place that had been frozen for a long, long time.

Her eyes opened to meet Ben's and were held by the troubled look she saw in their grey depths.

"*¿Mucho calor?*" he asked, his voice quiet and intense, his lips close to her ear. Maria could only stare up at him, dismayed herself at her physical reaction to his touch.

"Do not!"

"Do to!"

"Do not!"

Their attention was abruptly brought back to the children, a squabble escalating between David and Trisha, Maria's oldest girl.

"Mama, will you tell this moron that he has to study Spanish or he's denying his cultural heritage." The phrase sounded odd coming from the child's mouth, but her serious expression showed she was in earnest.

"Well, I don't know about that," Maria said, freeing herself from Ben's arms to sit on the grass beside him, "but I think it's important that you're bilingual."

"See! Bilingual means you speak two languages, you dope."

"What do you know?" her cousin retorted. "You don't know nothing. You, you—you *secretary!*" He spit the vile word out.

"That's enough." Their grandmother's voice cut through the air. The children silenced immediately at the order but continued to glare at each other. "I think we'll learn the Spanish words for 'mop the floor' and 'clean the bathroom' since you seem to have so much energy this afternoon. Come! All of you!" Their grandmother was not to be disobeyed, but the children groaned anyway as they trooped into the guest house, the old woman a formidable presence at their back.

"Secretary?" Ben questioned after the door had shut behind them.

Maria settled back against the trunk of a cottonwood and began to pluck absently at a stem of grass. "David's father left my sister, Linda, for his secretary. She's pretty bitter about the whole thing, and 'secretary' has turned into a dirty word at their house. I don't think he even knows what it means, exactly, but he figures it's bad."

"Poor guy. Does he see his father much?"

"Every other Saturday. But the secretary's already pregnant, and he 'forgets' to pick David up about half the time." She saw Ben wince at the controlled tone of her voice and knew she hadn't managed to mask the violent anger she felt against the boy's father. They were silent a moment, the late-afternoon sun warm on their faces.

"How'd you like to go to Wyberg tonight and see a movie?" Ben asked suddenly, startling her with his abruptness.

"Why, that would be wonderful. The kids would love it."

"I meant..." Ben stopped. "Sure, the kids will have a great time. It will do us all good to get into town for an evening."

Maria knew he hadn't meant the invitation to include the children, but she also knew she would have trouble forgetting the way her body had felt on top of his just a few moments ago, the way his lips had tasted... The children should definitely come.

"I'll go tell them." Maria got up and brushed her hands over the seat of her shorts, aware that Ben's eyes followed the movement. "Do you want me to ask Connor, too? I know he goes into town almost every night, but he might want to come with us."

"I doubt it, but you can check. It could be Veronica will be enough lure to get him to spend an evening in my presence." Ben smiled when he said it, but Maria saw the pain in his eyes. The way Connor avoided him was so obvious it was painful for them all to watch.

"You go tell the troops we're hitting the bright lights tonight, and I'll try to get some work done before supper." Ben pulled himself up, slapped his hat on his head, and started for the barn. Maria watched him cross the yard and disappear into the shadows of the barn, a strong, capable, confident man who would rather wrestle a mountain lion than approach his own son.

Maria knew how he felt as she walked up the stairs to Connor's room a few minutes later. Except for a grudging admittance once a week for cleaning, Connor's room remained off-limits to the rest of the household. It was never anything actually said, but the way he carefully and deliberately kept his door shut made it obvious, even to the children, that his privacy was sacrosanct.

So when Maria reached his room, she was surprised to see that the door stood ajar. The breeze blowing in from the window at the end of the hall must have pushed it open.

"Connor?" She tapped softly at the half-open door. She could see the boy hunched over a paper-strewn desk, working intently.

Connor's head snapped up at the sound of his name. His hands instinctively covered the paper he was working on.

"May I come in?"

"Sure."

"Your dad thought we might all go into town and see a movie tonight after supper. You want to come?"

Connor shrugged. "I've got some things to do around here."

"Maybe they could wait until tomorrow? I know Veronica's really looking forward to going."

Apparently, the outing sounded a lot more interesting all of a sudden. "Well, I guess I could go." He nodded. "Sure, count me in."

"Great." Maria smiled and was rewarded by Connor's answering smile. He really was a handsome young man, she thought, when he stopped being so self-consciously belligerent. A sudden gust of wind pushed open the door to the room even wider and swirled among the papers on Connor's desk, lifting them up and scattering them to the floor.

"Uh-oh, let me help." Maria crossed the room and knelt to gather up the sheets. They were thick pieces of drawing paper and she couldn't help but look at what was on them. The pictures were all done in pencil, black-and-white drawings of incredible detail. Maria's hands stilled and she stared at the papers she held, turning them upright so she could study them. There were unicorns and castles and butterfly wings, wolves with eyes that burned, delicate cactus so intricate she could see the fine hairs at the ends of the spikes. She lifted her eyes to meet Connor's where he sat frozen at his desk.

"Don't tell Dad," he ordered, panic in his voice.

"Don't tell him what? That you draw these incredibly beautiful things? You've got to be kidding!"

"Promise me!" Connor's face was pale. He was definitely not kidding.

"But, Connor, your father would be so proud of you! You have an amazing talent. He'd—"

"Dad wouldn't understand," Connor interrupted. "All he understands is cows and horses and fences and sagebrush." The words were bitter.

Maria looked down at one of the drawings she held, a picture of a sagebrush with its leaves deceptively fragile against its sturdy stem. "I think you understand those things pretty well, too."

He grabbed the papers out of her hand. "Promise me," he repeated.

"Okay, Connor, I promise. I won't tell your father." Maria gathered the rest of the papers and stood, placing the stack on Connor's desk. Her glance was captivated by what she saw there. Connor had moved his hand off the picture he had been working on when she came in, and Veronica's face looked back at her. Her sister was laughing, her dark hair loose around her shoulders, looking young and beautiful and completely naked from the waist up.

Connor paled even more and quickly turned the sheet of paper over.

"That was beautiful," Maria said gently. "I've always thought doing portraits must be very difficult."

Connor just sat in miserable, embarrassed silence.

"Well, I'll tell your father you'll be coming with us tonight. I know Veronica will be pleased. She really misses her husband." Maria felt a deliberate reminder of Veronica's marital status was appropriate.

But at her mention of Roberto, Connor tossed his bangs in disgust. "That jerk," he said.

"Roberto's a nice guy, really," Maria said mildly.

"He doesn't even call her. What kind of a husband's that?"

"It's expensive to call from Tucson. He's probably trying to save every penny for when he starts college in August."

Connor looked unconvinced.

Maria shrugged. "Marriage can be difficult. But I'm sure Veronica and Roberto can work out any problems they might have."

"Doesn't look like much of a marriage to me. Not that I've ever seen one that was."

Maria wasn't surprised by his cynicism. She was sure he spoke from experience.

"Shut the door on your way out." Connor made a show of picking up his pencil and starting back to work.

"Right. Supper will be ready in an hour. I'm making your favorite chicken enchiladas." Maria didn't expect any polite noises of appreciation. She made sure the door was tightly shut behind her.

* * *

"We want to go with Connor. We want to ride in Connor's car." The children clamored around the red sports car, oblivious to the young man's frown. "There's not room for all three of you in the back seat."

"Sure there is," Veronica said. She opened the passenger door and leaned the seat forward. "Get in, you guys. And don't touch anything."

"We won't," they promised in unison.

Ben saw Connor's face fall as the boy watched his car fill with children and his plans for sixty miles alone with Veronica turn to dust. With a glum look, Connor got behind the wheel and started the engine.

"I guess that leaves just you and me," Ben said, turning to Maria where they stood in the driveway.

"I guess so." Maria walked with him around the truck and waited while he pulled open the door for her. "Poor Connor," she said with a half smile.

"It's safer that way," Ben said. But as he helped Maria into the high seat of the pickup and slammed the door, it was his own safety he now worried about. Sixty miles with a woman who could boil his blood with no more than a brief touch of her lips? Not safe at all, he thought, thumping the tailgate uneasily as he rounded the truck.

"Goodbye, Señora Romero," he said to the woman who stood on the grass holding the baby, watching their departure. "Enjoy the peace and quiet. We shouldn't be too late."

"Take your time. You young people need to have some fun." She looked on benevolently.

"Oh, Señor Ben." Her voice caused Ben to turn, his hand poised on the door handle, eyebrows raised in expectation. "Remember," she said in a low voice, for his ears alone, *"mucho calor."* Their eyes met. *"¿Cuidado, no?"*

And Ben, even with his rusty Spanish, understood exactly what she meant.

"Too bad, Connor, it looks like you're out of luck tonight," Ben told his son as they studied the marquis above the popcorn counter. "We've got Walt Disney to our left or women crying to our right. What do you think?"

Veronica and the children had already decided on the new Walt Disney cartoon, and Connor gave in with fairly good grace. "At least Disney's got some pretty cool villains. It's got to be better than that tearjerker."

"How about you," Maria asked Ben. "Cool villains or tearjerker?"

"Tearjerker," Ben chose without hesitation. "Singing cartoon animals make my teeth ache." He turned her toward the double doors to the right and propelled her ahead. "See you later, kids," he called over his shoulder. "Meet us by the water fountain when your show's finished."

Maria had appeared to enjoy the movie, sniffling in all the right places, but Ben had been unable to concentrate. Driving home, the desert passing unseen in the dark, Maria's presence was as distracting as it had been in the ancient theater. He was just as aware of her body clear on the other side of the truck's cab as he had been when she sat only inches away in the worn velvet seat, the smooth skin of her arm tantalizingly close on the scarred wooden armrest. Her delicate scent was as disturbing now as when it mingled with the aroma of buttered popcorn and licorice. He wanted to glance away from the road to look at her, just as he'd been unable to keep his eyes on the screen.

Cuidado, Ben reminded himself, gripping the wheel. Careful. Mrs. Romero had seen the dangers and thought to warn him. He had so many things to be careful of. His relationship with Connor deteriorated with each passing day, and his delight in Maria's daughters grew with matching speed. Their open pleasure in his company, their simple affection, the way their little hands would tug at his as they dragged him off to show him some latest project—all were a balm that soothed the wounds Connor could inflict with such unconscious skill.

He turned off the main road and guided the truck down the lane to the ranch house, the sight calming as always. He loved this ranch, the horses content in their pasture; the spring rains had left the grass thick and tall. The night was brilliant, the crescent moon enhancing rather than competing with the explosion of stars. The desert smelled clean and empty. He watched the cool air coming through the open window play with Maria's hair. Stray wisps from her braid caressed her cheek. Ben wanted to reach out and smooth the strands back, follow the curve of her cheek with his thumb... *Cuidado.*

"You're awfully quiet," Ben said. "Did that movie depress you? The dog was the only thing left alive by the end. I kept waiting for him to get the next terminal illness."

"But he did," Maria insisted. "Don't you remember the way it showed the skunk's mouth right after it bit the dog? That means he's going to get rabies."

"No! You're kidding. Even the dog's going to die?"

Maria nodded. "You mean you didn't even notice? The camera zoomed right in on that skunk."

"I could barely follow the plot what with all the sobbing and nose blowing all around us. And you couldn't understand a word the actors said talking around those respirators with all those tubes down their throats."

Maria laughed at his grumbling. "It wasn't that bad."

"Almost. And besides, I was distracted."

"By what?"

Ben looked at her, long and hard, and even in the dim light of the dashboard Maria could read the message in his eyes. She knew. She felt the same.

She sat very still while Ben turned the truck into the gravel driveway and switched off the lights and the key. They sat in the dark, not speaking, listening to the sounds of the cooling engine, the crickets, their own breathing.

Ben's look had shattered the peace of the drive. Connor had taken Veronica and the children to get ice cream after the show, so there was at least a half hour before everyone arrived home. She took a deep breath. "Would you like a cup of coffee?" Maria asked, her voice unnaturally bright.

"Sounds good," Ben replied, but she could hear the strain behind his words. He opened her door and escorted her into the house.

Maria fussed with the coffee in the kitchen as long as she could before she took the cups into the living room. Ben patted the couch next to him and Maria sat down, very straight, her cup clutched between her hands. The air vibrated painfully, so full of tension Maria felt it like another presence wedged on the cushions.

With a feeling of inevitability, she watched Ben sit his cup on the coffee table and reach for hers, placing it on the polished wood. Slowly, he lifted a hand to her face, to her cheek, tracing her jaw down to her chin, her throat, curling his fingers inside the collar of her shirt. He tugged, pulling her to him. Maria didn't resist—couldn't resist.

His lips touched hers, slowly, sensuously, not a frenzied adolescent joining but a mature sigh of homecoming. They tasted and tested and touched, savoring the feel, the texture, the essence of each other. She felt him undo the ribbon at the bottom of her braid and slowly run his fingers through the entwined strands, separating them, caressing them with his palm. He pushed her back so she half lay against the cushions with the dark mass of her hair fanned around her head, her face porcelain pale in comparison. She ran her hands up his arms, around his shoulders, down his back, delicate strokes of exploration. She luxuriated in the feel of his hands outlining her body in the same way, while his lips traveled the planes of her face and the curve of her neck, igniting her.

The knowledge that their families would return soon, that in a matter of minutes they would have to stand, tuck in their shirts, smile politely and walk away from each other, only intensified her feelings. A lifetime's worth of physical yearning compressed itself into the present. Maria was greedy, she wanted more. She held Ben tighter, closer, pressing herself against him and cursing the thickness of denim. She moaned when he gathered her cotton blouse up over her breasts, pushed the lace covering aside and lowered his lips to nibble and suck and tease. The shadow of his beard scratched against the sensitive skin of her stomach, the contrast between its roughness and the velvety inside of his mouth making her gasp.

They heard the crunch of tires on gravel. Ben groaned in frustration. He rested his forehead on her stomach and Maria stroked his hair while they waited for their breathing to calm, soothing him and her at the same time.

Sanity returned with the calm. Her hand stilled and, instead of stroking, began to push Ben off her. Neither spoke as Ben sat up and she struggled upright. She smoothed her shirt down and pulled her hair back into its ribbon, her movements awkward. Maria could feel heat warm her face, a heat that only moments before had warmed her body, and knew she blushed. Ben walked with her through the darkened kitchen to the back door, each careful not to touch each other. Without a word, Maria quietly slipped out the door.

* * *

Maria straightened the kitchen the next morning, Harvey and Ben eating breakfast at the table behind her. She ran the dishcloth around the burners on the stove, aware of Ben's eyes following her as she worked. They made her clumsy. Except for a polite greeting, they hadn't spoken to each other, and Maria was relieved Harvey seemed happy enough to fill the silence.

"Another great breakfast, Maria," Harvey said as he carried his plate to the open dishwasher. "Takes a man clear through to lunch." He balanced his plate in the rack and dropped his silverware into the holder in the door.

Ben followed suit. "It was delicious," he agreed. He stood beside Maria at the stove. She was surprised to feel his hand on the small of her back. "We'll have lunch at Harvey's today since we'll be working on that side of the ranch. Don't fix anything for us."

Maria nodded. She wanted to press back against the warmth of his hand, to turn and curl into his arms. Instead, she continued to wipe the top of the stove.

Ben waited, silent, until Maria was forced to raise her head and meet his eyes. What did he want? she thought desperately, trying to find some clue in their gray depths. How was she supposed to act the morning after? Like it hadn't happened? Like it hadn't been a mistake? A complete, total, stupid mistake?

But Ben's eyes were inscrutable. They gave away nothing of his feelings. He raised his hand to her face and his callused thumb brushed against her lips, outlining them for a brief, fleeting moment. Then he picked up his hat and strode out the door, letting the screen bang behind him. Harvey, who'd been staring wide-eyed at Maria, scurried after him.

"Well, well, well," Maria heard the old man say, his voice clear in the cool morning air. "Well, well, well! And don't go telling me to shut up, Ben Calder. You think I didn't notice nothing going on in there? If you think I'm going to shut up about this, you've got to be crazy. I'll wear you down. It's going to be a long hot day. I'll keep at you like a red ant after a dead fly. You'll be begging to tell me. I'll..."

Maria couldn't help but smile, although it was quick to fade as she watched them walk away.

Ben had worked late, another fence had been down near the highway. He'd arrived home, exhausted, just in time for supper and then he'd hurried to take a shower. He frowned as he pulled on clean jeans and wiped a towel over his wet hair; he'd done nothing but run in circles all day. He buttoned his shirt, pulled a comb through his hair and headed down the stairs, trying to forget the weariness and aching muscles the shower had done little to ease.

"Hey, there, ladies," he greeted Tina and Trisha at the bottom of the stairs. The girls were heading into the living room, one with a broom and the other a dust rag. "Isn't it a little late for cleaning?"

"Mama let us play today." Trisha told him. "She said she was too distracted to do housework so we could do it tonight, instead."

"Oh, she did?"

They were interrupted by Connor coming down the stairs, taking them two at a time. He brushed past them with barely a grunt and went into the living room. Ben heard the television come on.

"I'll let you two get to work, then," Ben said with a smile. He waited for them to enter the living room and glanced around the corner. The broom was so long Trisha had trouble dragging it across the wooden floor, and Tina seemed more intent on spraying the furniture polish than on wiping it back up, but they chattered happily as they worked.

Their childish pleasure contrasted painfully with the bored expression on Connor's face as he stared vacantly at the television. Ben's smile faded and his weariness deepened when he looked at his son. Trisha moved to the couch and struggled to sweep around Connor's feet; the boy didn't even bother to lift his shoes out of the way.

"Will you guys keep it down?" Connor demanded. "I can barely see the picture on this scratchy old black-and-white thing. I'd like to be able to hear it, at least. And sweep somewhere else."

Trisha's lips quivered and she took a step backward. Something inside Ben snapped, a physical sensation of pain.

His boots made a deliberate click on the floorboards as he strode to the oak gun case next to the bookshelf. He dug in his pocket for a ring of keys, quickly sorted through them and unlocked the case. He pulled out a .22 with a polished wood handle, grabbed a handful of shells from a small drawer on the side, then locked the case again.

He placed his formidable bulk directly in front of the television and slapped his large hand against the button, fading the screen to black. "Take it outside."

"What?" Connor's eyes were wide, the girls' even wider.

"Take this scratchy old black-and-white, no-good TV out behind the barn. Now."

Connor didn't argue with that quiet, quiet voice. He pulled the plug from the wall and lifted the portable set from its stand. He stood uncertainly in the middle of the floor, the television in his arms. When Ben turned and walked out of the room, Connor and the girls followed, Trisha trailing the broom behind. Ben went down the hall and through the kitchen.

"Girls, stay here with your mother."

The girls ran to Maria and clutched her legs. The broom dropped to the floor. Ben pushed the screen door open with such force it slammed into the side of the house. Maria jumped and held the girls to her. She tried to catch Connor's eye but he stared straight ahead at his father's back, his face white.

She watched through the screen as the two walked across the yard and disappeared behind the barn. The sound of the rifle and the explosion of glass were almost simultaneous. The girls held Maria's legs even tighter. Ben came back into view, rifle firmly in his hand. Connor again followed behind his father, but now his arms were empty. They marched back up the steps and into the kitchen.

"Go gather up all your tapes and CDs and those damned headphones," Ben ordered. "And that tape deck radio thing."

"No way!" Connor's white face blanched whiter. "No way are you going to shoot my tape deck!"

Ben went into the pantry and returned with a cardboard box. "Put them in here. We're mailing them back to your mother." He shoved the box into his son's chest. "From now on you're riding out every morning with me and Harvey. For the rest of your *vacation* you're going to be so sore and so tired and work so goddamn hard on this ranch, you're not going to have time to watch TV or do anything else."

Connor flipped back his bangs and lifted his chin belligerently, but his eyes were filled with tears and his voice shook. "Sure, I'll pack my stuff—and take it back home with me! I'm leaving. I'm going home." He rushed from the kitchen and headed upstairs.

"Fine, go!" Ben shouted after him. "But you're not leaving until morning. You're not going to drive in the dark when you're upset."

"Fine! You'd probably shoot me if I tried to leave now, anyway." Connor reached in his pocket for his car keys and threw them at his father, then he stormed up the rest of the stairs. The slam of his bedroom door reverberated through the house.

A heavy silence followed as Ben stared blankly at the keys in his hand. Maria's heart went out to him. She crossed the hallway and stood beside him, but he didn't seem to notice she was there.

"I'll get the kids ready for bed," Maria said finally, feeling helpless. She laid a hand on his shoulder, a brief touch, then left him standing stiff and silent at the bottom of the stairs.

Maria waited for him on the porch, nervously pushing the swing back and forth. The girls had been subdued and their mood had infected David; they'd gone readily to bed. Veronica and her mother had found reasons to stay inside, tactfully leaving Maria and Ben alone. But Ben didn't come. Maria glanced at her watch again, undecided. The smart thing to do would be to go to bed, to lay down on her unyielding cot and try to forget the feel of Ben's lips on hers last night. That would be the smart thing to do. The stupid thing to do would be to relive every touch of his hand, every warm breath on her skin, every stroke of his tongue—

Good Lord, how had she let a man make her so stupid? She had no business getting involved with a man—especially her employer—especially on a job that would last a grand total of three months. She wanted nothing to do with some quicky holiday romance. Unstable. The whole situation was unstable. A man might revel in that kind of short-term excitement, knowing he could walk away unscathed when it was over, but Maria would be damned if she was going to be the one left nursing a broken heart. This attraction could only end in pain all the way around. And men had caused her family enough pain to last her a lifetime.

But tonight Ben was the one in pain, she reminded herself. She stared at the windows of the house next door, waiting for some hint of movement. But the house remained still, deceptively peaceful, giving no indication of the churning emotions of its two occupants. The rich textured darkness of the summer night felt flat-black to Maria as she imagined Ben and Connor, each fortressed at separate ends of the house, neither with any idea how to breach the walls they'd helped each other build.

Maria jumped up so suddenly the swing bounced back and caught her painfully behind the knees. She couldn't stand it any longer. Ignoring her scraped skin, she ran across the yard and into the main house. The dim glow from the study, the only light in the brooding house, guided her to him.

She found Ben at his desk, elbows on its top, his forehead resting on the back of one hand. In the other hand he dangled the car keys, absently running a finger back and forth over the grooves and dips of the keys, deep in thought.

"Ben?"

He looked up. Maria saw him try to focus, to pick her out of the shadows of the doorway.

"Is there anything I can do?"

He shrugged.

"Want to talk about it?" She pulled a chair up close to the other side of the desk and sat down, leaning toward him in sympathy.

He shrugged again. "I don't even know what to say anymore, or what to think. Connor and I have been going downhill fast these past couple of years."

She waited for him to go on, patient; she had all night, or however long he needed. He didn't meet her eyes, just stared at the keys in his hand.

"I didn't much care when Lori took off with her used-car salesman," he began. "She hated the ranch, always had. Hated the long hours, the bad road, the isolation, the weather... Hell, you name it, Lori hated it. By the end, I was glad to see her go." Ben sighed. "But she took Connor with her, and I shouldn't have let that happen. I just didn't realize what it would do to us. I just didn't know..."

Maria looked closely at Ben. The new tone she'd heard in his voice was reflected in his face. Always before, Ben's worries about Connor had been tinged with a large dose of anger overlaid with something close to impatience. Now there was only sadness, sadness in all its aspects—regret, hurt and, most of all, a deep, soul-stripping weariness.

"I don't have a clue how to fix this one, Maria," he said. He threw the keys onto the desk with a jarring clatter. "These six weeks are our only real time together except for a few weekends here and there. But he's miserable, I'm miserable—" He stared over her head into the darkened corners of the room. "Damn," he breathed softly.

In that instant, Maria realized a number of things. She realized that she'd assumed Ben had divorced his wife. It had never occurred to her that Lori would have left him. In Maria's life, it was the men who walked out.

She also realized that Ben cared deeply for his son. On a rational level Maria knew a father must love his children just like a mother did, but on a gut level, she hadn't really believed it. The men she knew left too easily to care the way a mother did. She'd always thought her late husband had been the exception to the rule.

Most important of all, she realized that Ben was a good man. A good man, a good father, like Marcus. She ignored the whispered thought that Marcus had never made her heart race, her pulse pound, her blood sing. Ben was a good man, and she had a plan to help him. "I have an idea."

"What?" Ben smothered a tired yawn.

"You'll have to wait and see. Right now you need some sleep." Maria took Ben's hand and pulled him up. She lead him to the stairs and gave him a small push to get him started. "I'll see you in the morning."

Then, purpose in her steps, Maria returned to the study, grabbed the car keys from the desk and headed outside.

Chapter Five

Connor's shouts crashed into the kitchen and made Maria jump, even though she'd been expecting them. It was still very early. She was surprised he was up since he usually slept until at least ten o'clock. He must have wanted to escape while everyone was still asleep, Maria decided. She checked the biscuits in the oven, wiped her hands on a cloth, then hurried into the hall.

She met Ben running down the stairs, taking them two at a time, still buttoning up his jeans. He didn't even notice her, intent on reaching his son who yelled and cursed at the top of his lungs. Ben burst through the front door, Maria right behind him, a slight smile on her lips. She couldn't wait to see his face.

"My car! My car!" Connor waved his arms and hopped up and down in the gravel next to his red convertible. His duffel bag and stereo sat on the ground next to his feet. He spun around to face his father. "How *could* you? How *dare* you?" His eyes blazed at Ben, and Maria was shocked to see a look very close to hate twisting his face. She felt the beginning of unease stir in her stomach, and her faith in her wonderful plan faltered for the first time.

"What are you talking about?" Ben shouted back. "I didn't have anything to do with it! Maria!" he bellowed. He turned abruptly, not realizing she was behind him, and almost toppled her over before he could stop. He grabbed her shoulders to steady them both, but his fingers didn't let go when they'd regained their balance. In fact, they dug into her skin with a bruising strength.

"Did you— Don't tell me—" He took a deep breath and seemed to make a conscious effort to pry his fingers from her, holding his hands stiffly out from his sides. "Please don't tell me that you did this?" He jerked his head toward the car.

Pieces of Connor's car were laid out neatly on the grass next to the driveway. The belts and hoses made a tidy pile, the spark plugs were mounded on a piece of newspaper, the air filter, fuel filter, oil filter, water pump, every readily detachable section of the engine formed careful rows, an assortment of nuts and bolts next to each.

Maria smiled uncertainly. "I thought Connor might need a little something to do in the evenings now that he won't be watching television. My husband always said it was important to know your car inside and out." Connor and Ben stared at her with identical expressions of blank disbelief. "Marcus was a mechanic, you know, and he taught me quite a bit. And it's not like I can afford to take the station wagon into the shop very often. I'm pretty handy..."

Ben took a step toward her and Maria backed up, a reaction to the anger she saw on his face. "Just how did you expect all this to get back under the hood?" He had trouble talking through his clenched teeth. "You know Connor barely knows where the gas tank is."

"That's the whole point. Obviously, Connor is going to need some help putting it all back together. That's what's so perfect." Maria regained some of her enthusiasm. It was really such a good plan. "I thought it would be a perfect way for you and Connor to spend some time together, do something together."

Ben's face didn't reflect her enthusiasm. He looked madder than ever. "You told me you didn't want him to go," she reminded him, confused. "I thought—"

"You thought? You *thought?*" Ben's voice rose. "Did you give any thought to the fact that I'm so damned busy can't see straight? How the hell am I supposed to find the time to fix that mess? I don't have time to do engine jigsaw puzzles with that kid every night for the next two weeks!"

Maria stared up at Ben, stunned, absorbing his words. He had no time for his son. *No time for his son.* Maria felt a sadness so great, so overwhelming, she had no way to prepare for it. And, just as fast, anger ripped through her. A good man? She must have been crazy. Ben Calder was a man. Period. She should have known better.

She lifted her chin and swallowed her disillusionment. "Connor is here for only six weeks out of an entire year. If you don't have time for him now, when do you?"

"That's not what I meant. Of course I have time for Connor. It's just—" But Ben's voice trailed off, unable to defend himself from the disgusted set of Maria's mouth and the disappointment plain in her eyes.

Maria was more than disappointed. He was no different—no different than David's father, no different than her own father, no different at all. And the realization that he was not the man she'd thought, not the father she'd thought, deadened her very soul. "I'll have the car back together again by tomorrow morning, Connor," she said woodenly. "You can leave then. I'm sorry. I made a mistake. I have to finish breakfast now, the biscuits should be ready." Maria turned and walked slowly into the house.

"Damn." Ben hardly knew who to deal with first. "You—" He pointed a finger at Connor. "Go change into some boots. You're riding out with Harvey and me this morning. We'll work on the car for an hour after supper." He didn't wait to hear any protests, but stomped after Maria, mentally wording his apology.

It was an uncomfortable group that gathered on Maria's porch that evening. The night was hot and sultry, with black, ominous clouds piling ever higher along the ridge of the mountains. The wind had come up and it whipped through the top of the cottonwoods. The tossing branches creaked and moaned in irritating, endless movement that grated on Maria's nerves. She wanted to shout at them to shut up, but instead raised her voice at the children, reprimanding them with uncharacteristic sharpness whenever their horseplay became too loud.

She avoided looking directly at Ben where he leaned against the porch railing, a boot resting on the board that ran along the bottom. The wind ruffled his hair, pushing it back off his furrowed forehead. He stared at the mountains slowly fading in the gathering twilight and his frown was as forbidding as the massing clouds. He had apologized to her, and she to him, but it hadn't made things right between them. The words had seemed politely empty, inadequate to fill the chasm that had opened between them.

Connor sat on the swing next to Veronica, drooping with exhaustion. The day on horseback had taken its toll, and he twisted awkwardly on the wooden slats, obviously in pain. Connor was an expert horseman, but he hadn't been in a saddle for more than a year.

"We're spending some more quality time together," Ben had told them with a sarcastic bite to his voice when the women had shown surprise at Connor joining them. Maria had blanched at that, feeling the barb was directed at her. They'd all heard father and son yelling at each other while they'd worked on the convertible earlier that evening. After only fifteen minutes, Connor had thrown down his screwdriver and stormed into the house, and Ben had slammed the hood with so much force the windows in the guest house had rattled.

The children started to squabble again, and Maria gritted her teeth to keep from snapping. Ashley began to cry, fussy from the coming storm, sensing the tension in the adults around her. Veronica laid her, stomach down, across her knees and patted her back until the yowls faded into angry hiccups.

Tina ran up and threw herself onto Maria's lap. "They won't let me play. They're just being brats." Her voice went from whine to quiver. "I hate them."

"All right, that's enough." Maria hugged the tense little body. She knew the warning signs; her daughter was on the verge of a major temper tantrum. They all were, adults as well as children. "I've got an idea—why don't I tell you a story? How's that sound?" Tina snuggled against her mother, nodding, willing to be appeased.

"Come here, you guys," Maria called. "Story time." The other children piled on the ground at her feet and quieted down with a minimum of shoving and arguing. "What do you want to hear tonight?"

"A ninja story," David demanded immediately.

"Yuck." Trisha made a face.

"We had ninjas last night. How about Snow White?" Maria forestalled David's objections. "I'll make the queen really wicked and disgusting, okay?'' Agreeing to the compromise, the children settled back to listen to the fairy tale.

Ben listened along with the children, unwillingly enjoying Maria's expressive storytelling, her voice suitably wicked when necessary, each dwarf sneezing, yawning or grumping according to his name. The children were enthralled, and even Connor was paying attention; the story seemed to take his mind off his sore backside.

"So the handsome prince bends down and kisses Snow White, right on the lips, and her eyes pop open. It's a miracle! His kiss has brought her back to life. All the dwarves cheer and dance around.'' Maria took Tina's hands and clapped them together and swung them back and forth like a cheering dwarf's. "Then Snow White sat up in her glass-and-gold bed and looked at the handsome prince who'd saved her. He immediately asks her to marry him, and, of course, she agrees.'' Maria's singsong, storytelling voice took on a hard edge. "He's a complete stranger, she doesn't even know his name, but she says she'll marry him. Must have been some kiss.''

"He's a prince, kiss or not,'' Mrs. Romero said. "That means he's rich, with lots of maids and a cook and servants. Snow White was no dummy. Compared to a bunch of dwarves, I say marry him.''

"I'd like a lot of servants,'' Trisha said. "I wouldn't care if I knew him or not, if he was a prince...''

"That's right,'' Veronica agreed. "You have to be practical about these things, kiss or not.'' The women all nodded and smiled, and those condescending smiles grated on Ben's nerves. He was heartily sick of hearing how worthless his sex was, even if only by innuendo.

"Come, *niños*, story's over. Time for bed.'' Their grandmother gathered the sleepy children, stood by while kisses were exchanged all around, then ushered them into the house.

Everyone in the family treated Mrs. Romero with the utmost respect, Ben saw as he watched her push the door of the guest house shut behind her with her walking stick. He'd come to like the dour old woman, but he knew she was most often the instigator of all the ridicule the women seemed to delight in. She wasn't only the matriarch of the family, she was like the head of a secret club that promoted the idea that men were no more than a necessary evil—irresponsible ne'er-do-wells who took a hike whenever the going got rough. And tonight that attitude irritated the hell out of Ben.

"Lord, you women can turn even a fairy tale into a lesson in man-bashing," he muttered in disgust.

"I beg your pardon?" Maria twisted around from where she sat on the steps and looked up at him.

"It's just a story, a kid's story."

"Maybe so," Maria agreed, "but there's something to learn, a moral, in almost all fairy tales."

"And the moral is always that men are jerks?" Ben demanded. "In Hansel and Gretel, the father's a bum for letting his kids wander off in the forest? Is that it?"

Maria shrugged. "At least Hansel and Gretel had a father. In most fairy tales, there's no father mentioned at all. I didn't write the stories, but if the shoe fits . . ."

"That's right!" Ben snapped. "That's right. I forgot. I'm a terrible father, and I should be so grateful to you for showing me how to spend time with my son." He gestured with a flung hand toward Connor who sat wide-eyed and silent next to a gaping Veronica.

"I never said you were a terrible father, Ben."

"Maybe not said it, but your every word, your every move, lets us all know just how you feel about men, about fathers." Ben glared at her. He had admitted to himself that there had been truth in Maria's words that morning about Connor, about not spending enough time with him, and he'd felt guilty all day. Guilty and hurt, and that made him want to hurt her in return. "It must be nice to be such a perfect mother," he said with icy sarcasm. "But you should give some thought to what you're doing to your girls. You're turning them into man-haters, you know. Ruining them, just like your mother did you."

"My mother? What's my mother got to do with anything!" Maria sounded outraged.

"I don't know what happened to your mother to make her so bitter, but it certainly affected you and Veronica, and the girls are just echoing smaller versions of the same bull."

"You want to know what happened to my mother?" Maria jumped to her feet. "I'll tell you what happened! My father walked out on us when I was nine years old, that's what happened. Not because there was another woman, not because there was anything wrong, but because Mama was pregnant again with Veronica and he couldn't handle it. He couldn't handle the responsibility of another baby, the responsibility of his *family!*"

Maria shook with anger. "He left my mother when she was pregnant and had two little girls to raise. Do you know how difficult it was for her to start her own business, to support all of us?" Maria stomped up the stairs and stood next to Ben on the porch, crowding him against the railing. "She'd been raised in a traditional Mexican family, where the men were the head of the house, where the men took care of the finances and the women took care of the children. Yet she started a restaurant and provided for us, *by herself*, for all those years. I am so proud of what she did! I admire her so much! And I will not stand here and let you say a damn word about her, do you hear me?"

Tears began to stream down Maria's cheeks. She brushed them away with a swipe of her hand. "And my girls don't need her or me to make them man-haters. All they have to do is look around them. One uncle runs off with another woman, another uncle hasn't seen his baby in over a month, every—"

Maria broke off, the gasp from the corner halting her tirade. Ben swung around to see Connor looking in horror at the baby Veronica held across her lap.

"That kid's yours?" Connor was on his feet in a flash and backed against the wall as if he'd just found out Veronica had the plague.

Veronica cuddled Ashley to her shoulder and wrapped her arms tightly around her, protecting her, shielding her from Connor's obvious distaste. Ben felt sick to his stomach at the pain he saw on the girl's face when Connor bolted off the porch without another word.

"See what I mean?" Maria watched the boy's departing back. Her anger seemed to have burned her tears dry. "Men are so devoted to the women they love, aren't they? Stick by them through thick and thin, don't they?"

Turning her back on Ben, she helped a pale Veronica to her feet and walked with her into the house. She shut the door and flicked off the outside light, as if Ben weren't even there, alone on the porch in the dark.

Maria lay on her cot against the living room wall and listened to the rising storm. Tree branches scraped against the roof like fingernails on a chalkboard, prying at the shingles. The wind swept down from the mountains, nothing to slow it but stunted pinions and cactus. It hit the cottonwoods ringing the house with a fury that had built uninterrupted over miles of open desert. She heard a sharp crack and knew a limb had snapped, unable to bend far enough, for long enough.

The rain began with a suddenness that made her jump and pull the covers closer around her shoulders. There were no warning drops, no light patter to prepare her for what was to come. It was as if the clouds had been pierced by the slashing lightning bolts and dumped their water in a single, drenching burst. The wind blew the rain against the windows where it ran down in sheets as if the whole house were submerging. It went on and on, no brief summer thunderstorm, and Maria felt the hypnotic surge of the storm begin to fade her to sleep.

It took a moment for her to separate the pounding on the door from the noise of the wind. Her name being called seemed to blend in with the rain, washing away into the night. A brilliant flash of lightning coupled with a roar of thunder brought her fully awake. Harvey was knocking on the front door.

Maria pulled on her robe and ran to open the door. Harvey stood on the porch, water pooling around him, dripping from the brim of his hat and the hem of the poncho that hung to his knees. "Boss sent me to ask if you and Veronica could come give us a hand." He had to shout to be heard. Another bolt of lightning made them both flinch. "The washes are starting to run. We've got to move the sheep to higher ground."

Maria immediately woke Veronica and told her mother what was happening. The two women put on jeans, sweatshirts and light rain slickers, the only thing close to stormwear they had brought with them. They ran with Harvey to his truck and crowded in next to him. Maria saw Ben's pickup already moving out of the yard, careering down the gravel lane to the main road. A flash of lightning outlined

Ben's and Connor's heads in the cab and the bed of the truck filled with the ranch's dogs.

Harvey kept up a continual muttered monologue as he drove. "Stupid damn sheep," he cursed. "So damned dumb they'll stand right there and drown if somebody doesn't tell their curly white butts to move." His gnarled fingers gripped the steering wheel and he leaned forward, peering to see the road during the split second the wipers made a pass. "Boss is going to shish-kabob me, sure as hell. I'm the one that said buy them sheep. I don't know nothing about no sheep, he told me. Diversify, I tell him. Last time I'll listen to that Fred down at the co-op. Diversify, my foot."

"What about the horses and cows?" Veronica asked. "Will they drown, too?"

"They've got the sense God gave a goose." Harvey snorted. "But even if they didn't, the horses are snug in the pastures up by the house and the cattle's already been moved to summer grazing in the mountains. They'll be just fine."

They swung off the road and bounced along a rutted track. Red dirt seemed to move everywhere, running down the middle of the road, sliding off the hills, carried away by rain that had no time to soak into the fragile soil. Maria couldn't see more than a few yards in any direction; only the red taillights of Ben's truck ahead of them gave her any grounding at all. The lights stopped moving and Harvey put on the brakes.

"Yup, boss, that's just where I think they'll be, too." Harvey nodded to himself, agreeing with the location Ben had chosen. He put the truck in four-wheel drive, spun the steering wheel and dipped off the track, churning mud as he plowed to the edge of one of the many gullies that crisscrossed the desert floor. He maneuvered so his headlights shone up one of the wide, deep depressions in the ground.

"Me and the boss think alike, that's for sure. Course, that means we think like a damn sheep, too."

Maria and Veronica got out and walked with Harvey to where Ben and Connor had parked, higher up, their headlights sweeping the entire width of the deceptively flat desert. Ben peered over the edge of one of the many wide arroyos that had been carved out by the infrequent rains. The eroded stream beds were usually dry, marked only by an increase in tamaracks and other thirsty plants, but tonight Maria saw at least a foot of swirling water rushing along the bottom, stirring up the red sand and sweeping it along.

She didn't see any sign of sheep anywhere in the brush-choked gullies. She moved closer to where Ben stood and leaned over. His hand closed on her arm and pulled her toward him. "Careful. These sides cave off without warning." His voice was an impersonal shout into the rain and once he'd moved her back a few feet he dropped his hand. Maria shivered, colder than ever.

Connor ran up and handed them each a flashlight, but even with them and the headlights from the two trucks, Maria wondered how they were ever to find a small white sheep in the pitch-black desert. A shrill whistle cut through the cacophony of the storm, and Maria turned in surprise to see Ben with his fingers raised to his mouth. The border collies that had been waiting patiently in the back of the truck bounded out and came racing toward them. The whistle changed in pitch, and the dogs veered to the left and plunged headlong over the edge of the wash.

In less than a minute, Maria heard excited barking. "Let's go." Ben waved his flashlight and they moved in the direction of the barks. The bleating of sheep could be heard now, coming from the darkness around them. Suddenly, four grayish lumps popped out in front of Maria, bleating in terror, while a collie nipped efficiently at their hind legs.

Another group appeared just ahead, then another. Maria immediately saw why Ben had needed extra hands. No sooner did a dog force a knot of sheep to scramble up the muddy bank to safety, than they would hear the call of the rest of the flock and try to rejoin them at the bottom of the treacherous arroyo they'd just left—an arroyo that filled with more water by the minute.

Maria followed Ben's lead and raced back and forth across the desert, trying to forcibly keep the rescued sheep huddled together on a tract of higher ground, a small rise that sloped up toward the foot of a canyon. Fighting the flock instinct was exhausting work, and Maria ran in endless circles in the ever-deepening mud. The truck's headlights gave deceptive light, making the desert a two-dimensional world of flat gray and black shadows. Rain pelted her face and made a mockery of her jacket. She looked at the luminous dial of her watch and was amazed to see they'd only left the ranch forty-five minutes ago. It seemed as if she'd been slogging after sheep for hours, probably because she'd chased each one a half-dozen times.

"Harvey, why did I buy these sheep?" she heard Ben shout as she joined the others to form a sort of human fence around the sheep they'd managed to cluster together.

"Cause wool prices were really high last year, boss." Harvey's voice could barely be heard over the combined noise of the sheep and the storm.

"How are they this year, Harvey?"

"Record low, boss. Can't hardly give wool away."

"Then how come I still have these miserable, stupid creatures when I'm a cattle rancher?" Ben swatted his hat at a straying sheep.

"Never know what prices will do next year, boss. Never know."

"I'm going to sell these damn sheep, Harvey," Ben shouted into the night.

"Smart move, boss," Harvey shouted back.

There was a flurry of activity as the dogs chased over more stragglers to join the growing number on top. Almost all of the sheep were out according to Harvey's quick count, and they remained huddled together much easier now that the majority of their flock was intact once again. Ben whistled and two dogs appeared at his side. He flicked his hand, and the dogs started circling the border of the flock, patrolling it with merciless nips.

"I think we're out of the woods," Ben yelled, and he gestured the group to leave their posts and join him.

Maria slogged toward him, her tennis shoes filled with mud at every step. She swung her flashlight in a wide arc, trying to avoid the cactus that ripped her ankles and the small sandstone boulders she continually banged her shins on. She raised a wet sleeve to wipe the rain off her face. Out of the corner of her eye she spied a woolly shape, an independent thinker, start to trot away from the flock in the direction of the gully. She headed for it and saw Connor move in its direction, as well. As if sensing pursuit, the sheep began to run. Ben joined in the chase.

The sheep made Maria rethink Harvey's opinion about the creatures' intelligence. It seemed to always be one hoof in front of them. If they moved to the right, it moved to the left; if they went forward, it went back. Ben and Maria guarded the sloping ground that led toward the gully, waving their arms and yelling crazily, while Connor tried to chase it back up to the flock.

Connor seemed to have unlimited energy and he'd been at a dead run the whole time. The hard day he'd spent riding with his father might have never been. Maria was amazed when, in a flash of lightning, she saw his face. He was laughing, shouting into the storm and kicking up mud as if it were a great game. She'd never seen him so uninhibited, so childlike, so joyous. Mud covered him from floppy bangs to unlaced tennis shoes, his eyes were pale circles in his mud-splattered face, and his teeth flashed white as he howled and leaped and spun across the desert.

Maria looked at Ben and found him watching his son's antics with a smile on his face. It was the first time she could remember seeing him smile at Connor. The sheep finally gave up and allowed itself to be guided back to the flock, Connor running behind. Maria followed, much less energetically, her progress slow up the slippery incline. Thunder sounded ominously in the distance, a rolling, roaring throb that made the ground tremor under her feet.

Dark, silent shapes sprinted past her. She watched in surprise as the dogs raced ahead, bolting for higher ground. She could still hear an occasional bleat from the arroyo and wondered why they weren't bringing up the last of the sheep. The thunder was louder now, and closer. Maria stopped and looked around, confused, but could make out nothing unusual in the desert shapes weirdly silhouetted by the truck's headlights.

Behind her, she saw that Ben had stopped, too. He listened, his head cocked at an attentive angle. Suddenly, he broke into a run. "Run! Run, Maria!" Ben's shout confused her even more, but she obeyed unquestioningly. Ben was beside her in seconds, he grabbed her hand and yanked her along with him. She stumbled but he didn't let go, dragging her a few feet until she regained her footing. The entire desert seemed to shake, to heave under her feet, and an incredible roar vibrated inside her body like a second heart.

Ben pulled her up the last few muddy feet to the rise where the sheep milled in renewed panic. Only the ever-circling dogs kept them from fleeing. Ben swung around and looked back the way they had come. Maria panted, her eyes frantically darting across the landscape for the unknown danger that bore down on them. The darkness seemed to grow, to swell, and a wall of water roared out of the night.

The rust-gray water filled the entire width and depth of the arroyo and clawed at the banks, greedy for an even bigger channel. Junipers and cedars were sucked out by their roots and tossed among the swirling water. Their branches instantly became crowbars that pried out anything that tried to resist the flash flood. Maria watched in horror as the moving wall reached Harvey's old pickup parked so close to the gully's edge. The sand melted from around its tires, turned to pudding. The truck slid gracefully into the water where the current rolled it on its side as effortlessly as a tin can. Its headlights bobbed drunkenly, weaving patterns in the sky, and the truck joined the debris that rushed helter-skelter downstream.

The power she witnessed overwhelmed Maria and she felt her legs tremble. Ben still held her hand, and she tightened her grip instinctively. Ben seemed strangely exhilarated by the dramatic display. He whooped into the night, a challenge, as if daring the chaotic, roaring mass to try to reach him. He laughed, so much like his son, and pulled Maria into his arms.

His kiss was a part of the elements that surged below them. It was raw and hungry and tore at her mouth, and Maria felt the earth under her turn to quicksand and shift, giving way to the force of his current. She was pressed against him, clinging to his shoulders. She knew she was drowning but was unable, unwilling, to save herself.

His lips were savage and wild and she let the passion flood over her while the rain ran down their faces and the wind tried to push them together and tear them apart. Maria's tears mixed with the rain and she didn't try to understand why she cried.

The water was gone as quickly as it came, settling down to fill barely a third of the now-widened arroyo and leaving behind piles of uprooted brush and trees. Maria was out of Ben's arms just as quickly. He released her, set her aside and, without a word, walked toward his truck. The flood seemed to have drawn the fury from the storm. The rain and wind slackened considerably in its aftermath, nature paralleling the same anticlimax that Maria felt when Ben left her.

Slowly, she joined the others. She slid in next to Veronica in the cab of Ben's truck. She didn't look at him and he didn't look at her. Connor and Harvey jumped in the back, and, using a combination of the truck and the dogs as shepherds, they led the sheep down to the road and across it to a fenced section where the terrain was less dangerous. Ben drove them all home—Harvey would spend the night since it was so late and he no longer had transportation. They quickly changed into dry clothes and met back in the kitchen of the main house for hot chocolate.

"She was a good friend," Harvey moaned to the group gathered around the table. He pushed back the sleeves of Ben's work shirt and accepted the steaming cup Maria handed him with a sad smile of thanks. He hiked up the legs of the jeans that bunched around his feet and sat down. "She was a good friend, Nellie was. Don't know what I'm going to do without her."

"She was a rusting piece of junk with 270,000 miles on her," Ben brutally reminded his friend. "And you were going to trade her in this summer."

"All those miles were honest, hardworking miles, though. Nellie was loyal, loyal as the day is long. A good truck." Harvey sighed. He let the cup warm his hands and, in spite of being inconsolable about his truck, wondered about the folks sitting next to him.

The boy wouldn't even look at pretty little Veronica, when before he never hardly took his eyes off her. And she had her chair turned so far away from him, she was just about backward to the table. And the boss and Maria were both stiffer than boards, and so damned polite, pussyfootin' around each other, it sat his false teeth on edge. Harvey took another sip of the sweet hot chocolate. Something wasn't right here.

"I'm sorry about your truck, Harvey," Veronica said, rising to her feet. "But it's after midnight and I have to get back to Ashley." Harvey saw her glance pointedly at Connor. "My baby needs me."

"I better get to bed, too." Maria jumped up as if the idea of being left behind scared her to death. Connor and Ben had their cups in the sink and were on their way up the stairs lickety-split. Harvey picked up his pillow and pile of blankets and headed for the couch in the living room, convinced, now, that something was very wrong.

Nobody had told him to shut up all evening.

Chapter Six

Ben took a deep breath, let it out slowly and explained one more time. "Water has to run through the engine to keep it cool, right?" Connor nodded. "But there's no reason for water to run through the air filter, a wet filter wouldn't work. So that hose can't go there. See what I mean?"

Connor looked at the curved piece of molded black hose he held, then he ducked back under the open car hood and studied the maze inside. He stared right past the gaping hole that cried out to be plugged by the hose he held, and Ben gritted his teeth to keep from yelling, "There! Don't you see? Right there!"

Finally, after what seemed an eternity to Ben, Connor hesitantly fitted the end of the hose onto the proper place on the radiator. "It looks like it might fit here, I think?"

"You got it." Ben's shoulders sagged in relief. He hadn't realized he'd been holding himself so tensely. They'd been working on the car for more than an hour, and his son's complete lack of mechanical aptitude had shocked Ben.

Some of his own happiest childhood memories were of tinkering with old toasters or radios or any broken piece of machinery he found in the scrap pile. The intricate mesh of gears, dials, wires and metal seemed close to art to Ben and appealed to his sense of order, of rightness. He found it almost offensive that his son couldn't see the obvious interrelatedness of the engine arranged with such logical purity in front of him, and instead saw only a jumble of what-cha-ma-thingies.

He watched while Connor clumsily tightened the clamp around the hose with a slotted screwdriver. Ben was making Connor put back every single engine item with his own hands, even though the boy was excruciatingly slow. They'd stopped work early today so they'd have more time to devote to repairing the car. It was taking much longer than he'd thought. He'd hoped that they would get all the belts replaced that afternoon as well, but it looked as if they would barely finish the hoses.

At least he hadn't lost his temper today, Ben thought. It was the first time since they'd started work on the engine four days ago that one or the other of them hadn't ended the job by hurling a tool to the ground and stomping off.

There'd been no further mention of Connor leaving. Every morning he'd rise at five-thirty and stumble to the breakfast table still half-asleep. As usual, he would be charming to Maria, condescending to Harvey and sullenly, stubbornly silent with his father. Then he would saddle his horse and join the two men, a third pair of hands to help with the never-ending chores of checking fence, caring for livestock, repairing equipment and irrigating the acres of pasture grass and alfalfa.

Connor had a natural ability with horses and working with them seemed to be the only part of his day that brought him any pleasure. He'd return in the evening, sunburned, exhausted and starving. He'd join them for a dinner that was tense and uncomfortable; only the children still chattered away unaware of the undercurrents. He studiously avoided Veronica and her baby and would escape to his room as soon as possible. Neither he nor Ben stopped by the guest house porch at night.

Ben had decided to give Maria and her man-hating family a wide berth. He'd known they were trouble the minute they'd driven up—he should have sent them all packing that very first afternoon. Ben missed his time with the children more than he'd thought possible, but it was better to break it off clean right now. It would hurt less all the way around. Ben was definitely not father-type material and he didn't need to be influencing any more young lives. Messing up with Connor was all the guilt he could handle. Besides, he knew Connor was perversely jealous of his affection for the children. Connor might not want anything to do with his father, but that didn't mean he wanted anyone else to be close to him.

And no children meant no Maria, which was just fine by him, he told himself firmly. His clumsy words when he'd found Connor's car had done nothing to endear him to her—had done nothing but confirm her already low opinion of men. That brief moment they'd shared after the movie was certainly not going to be repeated, she'd made that clear. And he was in perfect agreement. He'd spent the best part of the past four days trying to stop thinking about the way her hips had lifted to meet his as he'd pressed against her on the sofa; to stop smelling the fragrant mass of her hair as he'd buried his face in it—

Damn! He'd considered her attitude a challenge—and he'd never backed down from a challenge in his life. But he was from this one. *Mucho calor* was right. Maria Soldata was much too hot for him to handle.

A truck pulled into the yard and Ben glanced up from the shadowed depth of the engine, squinting into the sunlight. Harvey pulled up beside them in the dilapidated truck Ben kept to haul feed. Poor Nellie followed docilely behind pulled by a chain wrapped around her rusted front bumper. Her dented driver's side door was tied on with a piece of twine and the windshield reflected a mosaic of fractured glass. An inch of desert mud hid her faded blue paint and the branch of a scrub oak stuck through her front grill.

Harvey leaned his head out the open window of the feed truck and spit a stream of dark brown tobacco juice onto the gravel. "Hey, boss, can I ask you a favor?" He wiped at his mouth with the back of his hand.

"Sure. What do you need?"

"I thought I might ask Maria to drive into Wyberg with me to take a look at some new trucks. I gotta deal with those slick coyotes at Cactus Motors and Maria seems to know her way around an engine. Thought she might be a good one to watch my back in case they try to pull a fast one." Harvey pushed his hat back and scratched at his balding head. "Course that'll mean your supper will be a mite late tonight."

Ben shrugged. "That's all right. I think Maria's in the kitchen if you want to ask her."

But Harvey shook his head. "I've got mud up to my knees from fishing Nellie out. I don't think Maria would want me traipsing through her kitchen."

Ben hesitated, his reluctance obvious. "I'll go ask her for you," he said finally. He reached for a rag and wiped his greasy hands on it, then handed the rag to Connor. "Wipe off and call it a day. We're not going to get to those belts." Connor looked at the rag, stiff with black grease, then looked at his own grimy hands. Ben saw the distaste on his son's face, but he ignored the curled lip and headed for the house.

Maria covered her ears with her hands to block out the howling protests of the food processor as it beat the cream in its bowels into submission. Every morning she would carefully skim the cream off the top of the gallon jars of warm milk Harvey brought in. She had collected several quarts of the rich cream and had decided to try her hand at making butter. The high-pitched squeal was giving her a headache but she resisted the impulse to turn the machine off and lift the lid to peak. Ben had said it would turn into butter, the operating manual for the food processor that she'd found in a drawer had said it would turn into butter, so she had to believe that the frantically whirling white cream would eventually solidify into something resembling butter.

Maria was surprised at how much she enjoyed the work on the ranch. And the children thought it was the most wonderful vacation they'd ever had. Every morning they would search through the dim, musty henhouse for eggs, carefully lining them up in the empty egg cartons she gave them. Then they would dive into the haystack, tunnel through the barn, shuffle under dried leaves, ferreting out every hiding place the hens were likely to try. They would bring the eggs into the kitchen, triumphantly presenting them to her as if they'd found buried treasure and the crumpled cartons held gold nuggets.

Maria would send them out to pick whatever vegetables were ripe and they'd return with sun-warmed zucchini, which she'd rinse and add immediately to the pot of soup that simmered constantly on the back burner of the stove. They helped her flour cake pans, sifting themselves and the kitchen with a dusting of flour, then they'd clean themselves off by jumping into the pond and letting the cool mud squish between their toes.

They had sat around the steaming kitchen and pitted cherries until adults and children alike had been stained red to the elbows. Jars, rings and lids were sterilized and laid out to dry on towels spread across the kitchen table. Cherries were mashed and mixed with sugar and pectin, the jelly poured into pint jars, the date written on the shining gold lids with black marker. Cherries were dumped whole into quart jars, lids sucking shut with a sharp click when they sealed. Cherries were frozen in round plastic containers, stacked one on top of the other in the massive freezers.

Maria enjoyed the work, enjoyed her days, and that made the atmosphere in the evenings that much more unbearable. The adults at the table were so tense, her carefully prepared food tasted like sawdust. They spoke of only the most innocuous topics and everyone left the table as soon as possible. There were no more long coffee-drinking sessions, no nibbling at leftovers on the platters, no one brought out a pack of cards.

The timer buzzed and Maria jumped for the off switch, thankfully slamming it down. She took a moment to appreciate the blissful quiet, then pried off the rubber seal on top of the machine. The thick cream she'd poured in had been replaced with a sickly looking, thin blue liquid and whitish-gray clots. Whey and butter, if the manual were to be believed. Maria dumped the whole mess into a strainer and let the whey run into a bowl. She looked at the unappetizing clumps left in the strainer and reached out a tentative finger to poke at one.

"Butter."

Maria jumped as Ben's voice sounded behind her. She hadn't heard him come in over the noise of the processor.

"It looks disgusting," she said.

"Looks like butter to me."

"Not to me." She shook her head emphatically. "Butter is hard and yellow and comes in nice little rectangles."

"Stage dressing," Ben said. "But you can doctor it up to look like store butter if you want. Just add a couple drops of yellow food coloring and some salt." He shrugged. "Otherwise, throw that in the fridge and it'll be good enough for us." He sounded supremely indifferent to her household chores.

Maria dumped the butter into a small bowl and began to smooth it with a spatula to resemble the butter balls she'd seen wrapped in the freezer. Her lips tightened at the effort to ignore him as much as she could. He stood next to her with the same brooding manner he'd had all week, his eyes the stark, bleak gray of a winter storm, threatening snow. His cool stare made her movements jerky, and her awareness of his body close to hers made her hands quake so much she feared she'd drop the spatula.

"Harvey wants to know if you'll go with him into Wyberg to look at trucks," Ben said in the polite, remote tone he'd adopted with her. "He was pretty impressed with your work on Connor's car and thinks you'll be just the one to help him get a good deal."

His voice held no hint of sarcasm or accusation, but Maria's eyes narrowed at his mention of the car, as if hearing words he'd left unsaid. They'd scrupulously avoided the topic in the few tense, very brief conversations they'd had since the night of the storm.

"I'd be glad to go with him," Maria answered, just as politely. "When does he want to leave?"

"Pretty soon." Ben watched her cover the butter with plastic wrap. "I think I'll drive you in," he added, his voice casual.

Maria turned her head so quickly her ponytail swung across her shoulder and wrapped tendrils around her neck. She didn't bother to hide her surprise as she looked up at him. The past few days, he'd gone as far out of his way to avoid her as she had him.

But Ben didn't meet her eyes, just leaned against the counter and spoke to the air over her hand. "That old feed truck Harvey's driving wasn't really meant for highway speeds, and I need to go into the co-op anyway sometime this week. Might as well make it this afternoon." Now he spoke to his boots. "Can you be ready in half an hour?"

"All right." Maria nodded. "I'll tell Mama to start supper."

"I thought we'd pick up some pizzas and bring them back for everybody. Give you a break." His eyes met hers for the first time but they revealed nothing more than the formal concern of an employer for an employee. Maria might have never stood wrapped in his arms, oblivious to the rain, the wind, the lightning of the storm, her body molded to his while the flood shook the desert around them, while she shook inside at the primitive, hungry need.

She inclined her head the necessary few inches to indicate agreement. She kept her eyes downcast until she heard the tap of his boots as he turned and walked away.

The entire hour-long trip into Wyberg was accomplished without Maria or Ben saying a word. Harvey's nonstop talking made anything more than an occasional nod or smile unnecessary. Ben pulled into a parking space in front of the post office, and Maria slid across the bench seat after Harvey and jumped down to the pavement.

"I'll wait for you two at the co-op," Ben said, slamming his door shut without bothering to lock it. "Take your time.

I've got a big order and it'll take them a while to get it together."

"I bet Stella McClaskey will be happy to keep you company while you wait," Harvey said with a delighted cackle.
"I just bet she will." Still chuckling to himself, he took
Maria by the elbow and guided her up the sidewalk toward
the car dealership.

Ben watched them walk away. With her long, dark hair
caught up in a ponytail, her cutoff jeans, pink T-shirt and
tennis shoes, Maria looked like a teenager; only the added
curve of her hips and the confidence of her walk revealed
her maturity. Ben saw Tom Clark staring after her from the
front door of his hardware store, and he frowned as Tom
stepped out onto the sidewalk to follow her with his eyes.

"That your new housekeeper, Ben?" Tom called to him
with a friendly wave.

Ben nodded.

"Why don't you bring her by the store and introduce us?
Vergie was telling me before she left that you'd need some
canning supplies this season. I just got in a new shipment."
Tom's admiring glance stayed trained on Maria until she
disappeared around a corner. "Maybe I have something that
would interest the little lady."

"Don't know if we'll have time, Tom." Ben smiled tightly,
then spun on his heel and stalked off in the opposite direction.

Harvey's happy, satisfied whistle floated in the air above
Maria as they approached the farmer's co-op where they
were to meet Ben. A yellowed flyer advertising last month's
rodeo was taped on the window beside a certificate display-
ing a photograph of a little girl and a very large cow,
thanking the store for its purchase of the first-prize 4-H
steer. Maria walked through the glass door Harvey held

open for her, wrinkling her nose at the acrid combination of fertilizer, pesticide and leather that rose from the narrow aisles and dusty shelves.

She immediately heard Ben's voice coming from the back of the store. His deep baritone was followed by a feminine laugh that caused Maria's step to falter. She rounded an end display of shovels, rakes and hoes, and saw Ben leaning against the checkout counter, a lazy smile on his face. A blond woman in a purple tank top, cut low enough to reveal an expanse of freckled skin and a generous portion of cleavage, was half sitting on the other side of the counter, bent toward Ben, red-tipped fingers resting lightly on his arm. She laughed again, an intimate sound full of intimate memories.

"Stella, you're getting prettier every time I see you," Harvey yelled across the store. "I think I'll name my new truck after you. She's a beauty, too."

"Well, now, Harvey, that would be real sweet of you," the blonde said with an indulgent smile for the old man. "It was too bad about Nellie. We were all sad to hear about her getting swept away like that."

"Did you find yourself a new truck?" Ben asked.

"Yup. Got me a three-quarter ton, four-wheel-drive animal that'll go straight up a hill towing a boulder the size of a house. Had a picture of a truck doin' it right there in the brochure. And it's got air-conditioning and one of them fancy CD players, too."

Stella whistled. "Did Ralph give you a good deal on it?"

"Hell, Maria here had him eating out of her hand in no time. He said he cut off a thousand dollars just for the pleasure of meetin' her. Didn't hurt any when she pointed out that this one old nag he tried to pass off on me had a hole in the muffler and leaked oil like a sieve."

"Stella McClaskey, this is Maria Soldata," Ben intro-
duced Maria in an impersonal voice. "Maria's helping me
out for the summer until Vergie gets back."

"Pleased to meet you." Stella's smile was open and
friendly, and Maria tried to return it in the same spirit even
though the sight of the woman's hand still resting posses-
sively on Ben's arm caused a strange twisting in her stomach.

"I'm glad Ben's got somebody to help him out. He works
too hard." Stella practically purred up at Ben. "Ben, why
don't you come over to my house for supper sometime next
week? Maybe we can go dancing or something. We haven't
gone dancing in ages."

Stella's smile might have been friendly, but Maria knew
the woman's words were directed as much at her as they
were at Ben. She was asserting her territorial rights, staking
her claim against newcomers.

"I'll have to see about that, Stella," Ben replied with a
smile. "We're going to be moving the cattle from Purdy
Mesa over to Bell Canyon pretty soon. Don't think I'll have
much time for dancing."

Maria watched while Ben chatted with Stella a few more
minutes. He was relaxed and smiling, teasing her in an easy,
friendly manner. The twist in her stomach spread to her
chest. Although her anger with him had passed, her disappointment was a dull ache she couldn't seem to shake. She'd
actually started to think...things. To hope for...things. To
think Ben Calder might have actually been different. But in
spite of her disappointment, she missed her friendship with
Ben, missed their quiet evenings on the porch. Missed the
hoping.

"I'll pull the truck around back in a few minutes and load
up my order," Ben was saying to Stella. "I want to take a
look at this boulder-pulling wonder of Harvey's first."

"I'll be waiting for you." Stella's drawl held all the meaning any man could want, and Ben tipped his hat in acknowledgment before joining Maria and Harvey.

They walked the few blocks to the car dealership where Ben admired the new black truck. He hopped into the cab and fiddled with the CD player, pushing buttons and turning knobs.

Harvey stood beside Maria, looking at her out of the corner of his eye. He slit open the paper wrapper on a can of chewing tobacco with a stained thumbnail. "Stella's an old friend," he said, sounding casual as he took a pinch of the ground-up tobacco and stuffed it under his lip. "She's sure a flirt, though. Flirting's like breathing to Stella, she don't even know she's doing it. 'Course she wouldn't say no if the boss offered, but she knows by now he's not interested." Harvey patted Maria on the back, a fatherly gesture. "Wouldn't worry about Stella none," he said.

Maria smiled, the tight movement of her lips her only response as she tried to look as if she didn't understand Harvey's point. What did Harvey think she was worried about? she thought in dismay. What had her face revealed? Had Ben seen it, too? Frightened, Maria clamped down on her thoughts and turned away from where she'd been watching Ben in the truck. She tried to school her features to show only a mild, noncommittal interest.

"Looks like you got yourself a winner," Ben told Harvey, stepping down from the truck. "Are you really going to name her Stella?"

"Naw. Thought I'd name her Vergie. It'll give me pleasure to be giving orders to a Vergie for a change instead of the other way around. Take her for a spin?"

Ben shook his head. "We better be getting back home. Want to stop by the house for some pizza?"

"Thank you kindly, but Italian food gives me heartburn." Harvey lovingly took possession of the driver's seat, his hands caressing the steering wheel. "I guess you can take Maria home, then? I want to head over to the Blue Moon and show the boys my new Vergie."

"Sounds good." Ben and Maria waved as Harvey roared out of the parking lot, his grizzled face lit with pride.

Alone with Ben, Maria stuffed her hands in her pockets to keep from fidgeting uncomfortably. Harvey's words had made her so self-conscious she avoided looking at Ben. He started walking and she followed next to him, silent, back to his pickup. She waited in the truck while he helped the men load the coils of barbed wire, sacks of feed and boxes of veterinary supplies he'd purchased. She waited, too, while he stopped at a small restaurant on the way out of town to pick up the three large pizzas he'd had Stella order by phone.

Maria stayed pressed as close to the door as possible, the brown cardboard pizza boxes a fragrant barrier between herself and Ben. The door handle dug into her hip but she accepted the discomfort as somehow appropriate. The hour-long drive loomed in front of them and Ben didn't seem at all interested in breaking the silence. The late-afternoon sun drilled through the windshield, so Maria turned her head to watch the passing landscape through the open window. The only signs of life were an occasional white-tailed rabbit that darted frantically for cover, a prairie dog perched on its hind legs by the side of the road, sniffing for danger, a magpie screeching on a fence post. Twenty minutes with only the hum of the tires on the road reverberating through the cab was all she could take.

"This is ridiculous!" she blurted.

Ben merely raised an eyebrow.

"I can't go on like this," she said flatly. "It's making me crazy. Do you want me to quit? To go back to Phoenix? Do you want to find another housekeeper for the rest of the summer?"

"Of course not!" It was the first sign of emotion Ben had shown toward her in days, and Maria could see his shock was genuine. "Do you want to quit?"

"No, I don't. The kids love it here."

"And you?"

Maria looked out the window, away from him. She chose her words carefully. "I'm happy with my job."

"Good."

"But many more suppers like we've been having and Harvey's heartburn won't hold a candle to mine!"

"I'm all for calling a truce," Ben said, but his voice was neutral.

"A truce would be good—a cordial working relationship, employee to employer." She tried not to think how ludicrous that sounded.

Ben nodded. "All right."

"Good. Then we have to talk. To each other."

"All right."

Maria waited. The tires hummed, the pizzas cooled. She sighed. "Okay, I'll go first. How are the sheep?"

"Fine."

"And..." she prompted, after it became apparent that was going to be the extent of his contribution.

"And nothing. Sheep don't suffer psychological trauma, Maria. They didn't even know they were in danger. But they're not going to be my problem any more since I've sold the lot of them to Stella's brother. Let him rescue them next time."

"That's good," Maria replied. Now it was Ben's turn. His fingernails tapped on the steering wheel, and Maria could see him searching for an innocuous topic.

"I saw you got all the cherries canned. They look good."

Maria nodded. "I'll need some more quart jars and rings before I can put up the green beans next month."

Ben nodded.

This wasn't going well at all, Maria thought. They might as well talk about the weather next. One of them would have to bite the bullet and bring up a subject that mattered. She took a deep breath. "How are things going with Connor?"

"Fine."

Maria waited patiently this time.

Ben shrugged, aware of her silent goading. "Pretty much like you'd expect. He hates riding out to work with me and he hates working on the car with me."

"I don't think it's a matter of hating to do those things with you, but just hating to do those things period."

"Same difference." Ben shrugged again, as if unable to differentiate himself from his work or from the ranch.

"You know, I used to love working the ranch with my Dad." Ben's voice was low, almost as if he were talking to himself. "I'd beg him to let me skip school so I could ride with him. We'd saddle the horses and go check the fences, riding side by side looking for breaks, sometimes not saying a word to each other for half the day. But always glad to be together." Ben stared straight ahead at the road. "Connor and I never say a word, either, because he makes sure he rides as far behind me as he can so he won't have to talk to me."

He was silent for a moment, the brim of his hat shadowed his face. "I have no idea what that boy likes to do," he said, bewildered. "He's seventeen years old and, as far as I can tell, he never wants to leave his room!"

Maria wanted to tell Ben just exactly what Connor liked to do, what he did in his room, what he was so wonderfully gifted at. But she'd promised. There was little she could say to help Ben. "He's a teenager. It's a rotten stage to have to live through, for him as well as you. Give him time, Ben. He's a good kid. And he can be absolutely charming when he wants to be."

"Oh, I'm sure Veronica finds him charming right about now," Ben said in disgust. Connor's puppy love had died an instant death, choked off without a whimper at the first scent of responsibility. He now avoided Veronica as purposefully as he'd once pursued her. "I'm embarrassed, flat out embarrassed, by the way he's acting. Your whole family already thinks men are sewer rats, and Connor made sure he's swimming right down there with them."

"Veronica knew she was playing with fire when she didn't tell Connor the truth from the beginning," Maria said. "She's hurt, of course, but I really think she's just using Connor as a target for all her frustrations about her husband. And we don't think men are sewer rats," she added.

"Hmph," Ben shook his head. "After what you told me about your father, *I'm* beginning to think they are."

Maria smiled. "No, you don't. I've never met a man who loved being a man more than you. You're the last of a dying breed, remember?"

Ben returned her smile, but it was tinged with sadness. "I just might be, at that."

Chapter Seven

"Lunchtime, gentlemen," Maria called. She peered into the shadowy barn where Ben and Connor had spent the morning repairing tack and oiling saddles in preparation for the days next week they would spend on horseback moving cattle from one high mountain pasture to another. But there was no sign of them now, only the pungent smell of oil mixed with the scent of freshly strewn hay and the gleam of rich, warm leather hanging from hooks on the barn wall.

Maria heard David's excited laugh and her girls' answering squeals coming from the corral behind the barn. She followed the dirt floor through the center of the barn, past empty stalls, and pushed open the wooden half door at the other end, entering the sunlight again. It took a moment for her eyes to adjust to the light, and Ben was the first thing she focused on.

He looked devilishly handsome, like a cigarette advertisement, with a boot propped on the bottom slat of the corral and his elbows resting on the top slat. He wore a

aded blue work shirt tucked into tight jeans, a silver belt
uckle at his waist. His hat was pushed back and Maria
ould see his smile as he watched the children.

Connor had Trisha astride a small black mare, her legs
ripping the striped blanket covering the mare's swayed
ack. She had a handful of mane clutched in both hands
nd was laughing in delight as Connor led the mare around
he dusty enclosure. The mare followed Connor eagerly, big
ellow teeth nipping at the carrots he had stuffed in the back
ocket of his jeans, green tops waving tantalizingly in front
f her nearsighted eyes. Connor made a show of trying to
eep one step in front of the mare, twisting and zigzagging
o that she had to be more nimble on her old legs than she'd
een in years. Connor rewarded her occasionally by stop-
ing long enough for her to wrap her flexible lips around a
arrot top and tug it from his pocket. He'd stroke her nose
nd whisper into her ears while he rubbed them affection-
tely, then start the game again, the mare following like an
doring puppy.

"Time for lunch," Maria told Ben as she joined him,
tepping onto the bottom board of the corral and rising on
iptoe so she could see over the top rail.

"Good, I'm starving." He gestured to his son. "Did you
ver see anything like the way that boy has with horses?" he
sked her, never taking his eyes off Connor. "He's a natu-
al, has been since he was just a little thing. He used to ride
lmost every day when he was up here for the summer, but
he past couple of years he seems to have lost interest."

Ben clapped his hands to get Connor's attention. "Come
n, kids. Food."

The children jumped down from their perches on the
orral rails and raced toward the house. Connor gave the
aare the last of the carrots and removed the rope he'd used
o lead her. He left her chewing peacefully in the warm sun-

shine and ran after the children, the bored, slumping walk
he'd perfected momentarily forgotten. After a quick hand-
washing, they crowded around the big oak table in the
kitchen, reaching for thick sandwiches from the plate in the
center.

*Tina, you're going to knock over your milk. Get your el-
bows off the table. How was your morning, Señor Ben? We
got a lot done, Mrs. Romero. How was yours? I took a nap,
like an old lady should. Aunt Veronica, I think Ashley wants
a sandwich. Not yet, sweetheart, she doesn't have enough
teeth, you go ahead and eat all of yours yourself. But it was
nice of you to want to share. Can I have some more soup?
You're going to explode, David. I swear, your mother isn't
going to recognize you when you get home, you're growing
like a weed.*

Maria listened to the conversation, overlapping voices
rising and falling, the children's sopranos, Ben's low
chuckle, the cadence and rhythm of a family. She felt a
peace for the first time in days.

Maria was used to struggling, but she had learned there
were some things she couldn't fight, some things she had to
accept. She'd had to accept her father's desertion, her husband's death, the never-ending juggling act to make ends
meet, the constant weariness caused by long hours at the
restaurant followed by studying late into the night. She knew
this attraction for Ben was something she could not fight,
so she accepted it.

She accepted that she had had unrealistic, schoolgirl-type
fantasies where Ben was the kind of man she needed—a father for her girls, a friend and lover for herself, a strong,
dependable man who would have time for them all and who
would not leave. But Ben was just a man—and that wasn't
good enough. Physical attraction, no matter how strong,

asn't good enough for her or her children. And if that
ade her a man-hater, as Ben accused, then so be it.

Maria accepted her feelings and looked for peace where
e could find it. If an ache of longing came at night, when
e was alone in her cot by the wall, if her throat burned
ith needs she could not give voice to, then it made the
ace of times like lunch that much more precious.

She ladled more soup into David's bowl and sat down to
r food. "Move your horse braid off the table," she told
ina. The little girl obediently slipped the long brown string
to her lap.

"What are those things?" Ben asked. The children had
en carrying them around all morning, clutched in their
nds like talismans.

David pulled his out of the pocket of his T-shirt and
nded it to Ben. "Connor made them for us. Aren't they
at?"

Ben studied the strands of black, brown and gray horse
ir. The hairs were intricately braided in a spiraling de-
gn, and interwoven in the braid were bits of hollow sticks,
ny fluffs of feather and even small, shiny stones sparkling
ith mica. It was a delicate work of art and Ben dangled it
om his long, roughened fingers, looking at it with a puz-
ed tilt to his head.

"You did this?" he asked.

Connor nodded and shrugged. "The kids had fun col-
cting the stuff."

"Let me see the rest of them."

The children passed their braids across to Ben. He pushed
ack his plate and laid the braids out on the table, side by
de. Each one was unique, whimsical and reflected an
ormous artistic talent.

"Connor, these are amazing. They really are. I had no
ea..." Ben touched a finger to a feather, stroking it. "Did

you see what Connor made?'' he asked Maria, his voice
perplexed as if his son had developed a sudden talent for
Thai cooking or something just as exotic to his world.

"I saw them last night. I think they're beautiful." Maria
was aware of Connor's warning look, so she didn't add the
words she wanted to, praising his drawing, as well. The boy
smiled in embarrassment at his father's words, his face pink
as he basked in the admiration.

"I took this art class last semester called Mixed Media,"
Connor said. He pushed his bangs off his forehead with an
impatient hand and leaned forward eagerly in his chair. "We
did collages using all kinds of weird things, anything we
could throw together, clay and cloth and string and rocks,
just anything. I did a couple of pretty good pieces. My
teacher said I had real talent."

"I bet," Ben said. "Quite a talent. But, you know, what
you have a real talent for is working with horses." Ben's
voice was just as eager as Connor's. "I was telling Maria
I've never seen anyone as good as you are with horses. Now
that's what I call art."

Connor's glow faded and his faced closed with the
abruptness of a shutter slammed shut by the wind. Maria
wanted to kick Ben for being so dense, for being so completely absorbed in Calder Ranch that he only saw the value
in a skill as it related to the ranch. But Ben looked so bewildered by Connor's withdrawal when he thought he was
paying him the highest compliment that she wanted to hug
him, too.

The phone rang and Maria got up to answer it, shaking
her head in exasperation. It was her older sister, Linda. She
called twice a week from Phoenix to talk to her son.

"Is David handy?" her sister asked.

"He's right here eating lunch. David," Maria said, "it's
your mother."

"Wait, before I talk to him, I want to know when you're going to come down. The restaurant's starting to get pretty low on inventory."

Maria glanced at Ben. "I'm not sure. I haven't asked him yet."

"Well, ask soon. We're a lot busier this summer than we expected. We're going through supplies like crazy. I think it's those ads you've got in the newspaper."

"Do you need help?" Maria asked.

"No, I can still handle it on my own," Linda told her. "Besides, I need to keep busy. Everything's fine at your place. I'm watering your plants. And, good news, I've got a deposit down on an apartment that should be available in August."

"That's great," Maria said, pleased for her sister. "David's about to pull the cord out of the wall." She laughed. "I'll let you talk to him now." Maria handed the phone to the boy who was hopping about in excitement and sat back down at the table.

"You haven't asked me what yet?" Ben asked.

"Remember when you offered me this job, I told you I'd have to make two trips back to Phoenix during the summer to take care of the restaurant's paperwork and order inventory?"

Ben nodded. "I remember. Is it time?"

"It looks like it. I've been here over a month and Linda says business is better than we expected. She's running low on supplies. Of course she places the day-to-day orders herself, but I like to handle the major ordering. We can keep better control of costs if we order in bulk."

"When do you want to leave?"

"How about the day after tomorrow?" Maria started to stack the empty soup bowls. "It would be a quick overnight trip. I could leave early Thursday morning and come back Friday evening.'' She turned to her mother. ''Mama, could you and Veronica take care of things here until I get back? I could make a casserole ahead of time for supper.''

''I think I still remember how to turn on a stove,'' Mrs. Romero chided her daughter. ''I will make these men my special chicken tacos with my secret-recipe salsa so hot their eyes will weep with joy. David will help me. Mexican men are stupendous cooks.''

Maria gave her mother an appreciative look. She'd spoken to her and Veronica about Ben's accusations—that they were ''ruining'' the girls—and now they chose their words carefully in front of the children. David was having trouble enough dealing with his father's rejection—he didn't need to feel rejected, even subtly, by the women in his life, as well.

Connor helped Maria carry the dishes over to the sink. ''You know, Dad, I was thinking,'' he began in an offhand manner, ''like Maria said, we've both been here over a full month now.'' He started to load the dishwasher, a chore he'd never shown the least interest in before. ''This year I'm going to be up here for forty-seven days—that's really quite a bit longer than the six weeks I'm supposed to stay. I was thinking, maybe we could hurry up things on my car a bit and I could follow Maria back to Phoenix, make sure she got there safe.''

Ben's eyes narrowed and the look he gave his son was hard. ''You always stay until after we move the cattle.''

''I know.'' Connor kept his attention fixed on the dishes. ''But I thought since Maria was heading that way—''

''I don't think so,'' Ben interrupted. ''You'll help move the cattle, like always, and you'll leave after we come off the mountain, like always. We'll have your car ready by then.'' He scraped back his chair and picked up his hat. ''We'll stick to the plan. Round up the dogs and meet me in the truck in ten minutes. John McClaskey's got a semi coming his afternoon to pick up the sheep he bought. We better make sure they're ready and waiting for him.''

Connor stared resentfully at his father's departing back. He slammed the dishwasher shut, dirty dishes still piled on the counter, and left the kitchen without a word.

The sun was not yet visible, but its probing rays turned the sky over the mountains to the east a dusty peach. The mountains themselves were softened to a mauve smudge on the horizon, and a single, pristine white cloud floated above them, with edges so sharp, so distinct, it was as if a cotton ball had been glued in the sky. Maria looked at the splendor around her without seeing it. She stared out the windshield of the station wagon, her concentration focused on the grinding sound coming from the motor as she turned the key in her hand.

She took her hand off the key and waited. Sounds carried so clearly in the cool morning air she could hear the horses snort and whinny to each other from the pasture near the house. She tried the key again. The groaning was even worse this time, lower and more labored. The old station wagon hadn't been started since the day she'd arrived. She'd had no reason to go into town; Harvey bought the groceries from a list she gave him and did all the errands for the ranch. She'd had neither the time nor the inclination to drive the sixty miles into Wyberg during the past month.

Maria sighed. She got out of the car, retrieved the gallon can of gasoline she kept behind the back seat, lifted the hood and dribbled a small stream of gasoline into the carburetor. She heard the sound of Ben's footsteps coming across the lawn toward her.

"Priming the carburetor?" he asked.

"I thought I'd try that first. It might have dried out sitting here for so long."

Ben slid behind the wheel and turned the key again. "Nope. Battery?"

"It's new."

"Spark plugs?"

Maria frowned. "I could check. There's a socket wrench in the toolbox in the back. Could you get it for me?"

Instead, Ben got out, took the small red can from her and sat it on the ground. "I've got a better idea," he said. "I'll drive you."

"To Phoenix? You can't miss two days of work," Maria protested. "It's kind of you, but I can manage. I know this old tub inside and out. I'll get her started."

"There's some people I want to talk to in the city, anyway. Honestly," he said in response to her skeptical look. "I need to meet with my banker, and my lawyer's been wanting to take me to lunch for months. And I need a new pair of boots."

"Boots?"

"There's only one store in this state I'll let near my feet, a place in Scottsdale owned by a Polish man who can make leather feel like silk." Ben lifted the hood off the thin metal rod propping it up and dropped it with a loud clunk. He retrieved her battered suitcase from the back seat and crossed over to the porch to pick up the bag he had packed and waiting. "It was pretty obvious that old green monster wasn't going anywhere this morning," he explained in response to her questioning look. "I already told your mother I was taking you. Let's go."

Maria didn't protest further; she was too relieved to insist on her own way. She'd been dreading the drive, four hours with nothing much after Wyberg but rattlesnakes and cactus.

Ben stopped. "Wait a minute," he said. "I want to make a quick phone call first." He stepped into the house and dropped the bags in the hallway. The door, swinging shut behind him, caught on the bags and remained propped open. Maria couldn't help but hear his one-sided conversation coming from the living room as she waited on the porch.

"Lori?"

Maria stiffened at the name of his ex-wife.

"It's Ben. No, nothing's wrong. I'll be in Phoenix this afternoon and I wanted to see you. About Connor. No, he's fine. But there are some things I want to talk to you about." There was a long silence and Maria found herself leaning toward the door as if she could somehow hear the woman on the other end of the line. "Okay," Ben finally continued. "See you about three."

At the sound of the receiver being replaced, Maria moved down the steps. She couldn't imagine what Ben wanted to discuss with his ex-wife, and she wasn't about to ask.

"Ready?" Ben strode out the door.

Maria nodded. "Thank you so much."

"Sure. I'm already planning what I'll have for lunch on McGee, Ralston and Turner's account." Ben walked right past the truck parked in the driveway and headed for the garage attached to the back of the house. He raised the garage door to reveal a gray sedan, a big, powerful, luxury car centered in splendid isolation on the concrete floor.

Maria whistled. She looked down at her yellow cotton skirt, white tank top, and sandled feet. "I'm a little underdressed to be traveling first class. What's the matter with the truck?"

Ben opened the door for her and waited while she slipped into the seat to be enveloped by the plush upholstery. "Nothing's the matter with it. But there's no way I'm driving around Phoenix on the last day of June without air-conditioning."

"You have a point there," Maria admitted. She hooked her seat belt and settled back to enjoy the trip.

It seemed like much less than four hours had passed when they pulled into the parking lot of Casa Juanita, a small adobe-walled building with wooden vegas, black ornamental grillwork over the windows and doors and bright red geraniums spilling from terra cotta pots on the tile patio.

It was hard to maintain the friendly yet impersonal attitude she'd tried to adopt with Ben when he was only a few feet away—mile after mile spent glancing surreptitiously at his lean profile, noticing the way his brown hair curled slightly in back without a hat to push it down, wondering how he got the tiny scar on his jaw, studying his strong, tanned hands on the wheel, jumping slightly when he laid an arm across the back of the seat to stretch a cramped muscle.

By the time they reached Phoenix, she was feeling relaxed, even mellow. She had also discovered that Ben had hated his third-grade teacher, that he'd learned to braid a rawhide whip from his grandfather, and that he still missed his mother even ten years after her death. In turn, she'd told him all about the time she'd spilled punch on her confirmation dress, about her first disastrous Thanksgiving dinner for her in-laws, and how she'd always wanted a saltwater aquarium. How could you remain impersonal with a man when you knew he liked to suck the chocolate off candy before eating the peanut inside?

It was as if they'd left all their old animosity and misgivings behind with the ranch and were no more than a man and a woman—feeling the way a man and woman should feel.

So when Ben turned to her, the car's powerful engine still idling to keep the air conditioner fighting the noon heat, Maria felt a curious mixture of inevitability and hesitation.

"Thanks for the ride," she began when he failed to speak, just looked at her with sage gray eyes that were unclouded, relaxed and held just a touch of challenge. "What time do you want to leave tomorrow? I should be finished here by one or two o'clock, so any time after that would be fine. You can pick me up here."

"Two sounds about right," Ben agreed. "But I thought I might take you out to dinner tonight."

Maria could think of nothing she'd like better than to spend the evening with Ben. "That would be wonderful."

His smile heated her insides in a way the air-conditioning could do nothing to cool. Her fingers shook slightly as she wrote her address for him on the back of a grocery receipt she found in her purse.

"I've got a suite at the Glendale," he said, tucking the paper into his shirt pocket. "Their restaurant is first class if you like Italian food."

"Love it."

Ben's eyes locked with hers again. He seemed no more anxious for her to open the car door and step away than she was to do it, as if he, too, recognized the fragility of the cocoon they'd built over the length of the drive.

"Would you like to go to lunch with me?" Ben asked abruptly. "I'll cancel my lawyers."

"I'm—" She couldn't believe how tempted she felt. "I have to work, remember? The ordering. Linda's expecting me."

"Right. The ordering." He nodded.

She made a move toward the door handle.

"Here, let me get that for you." Ben jumped from the car and went around to hold open her door. The heat assaulted her like a physical blow, but all Maria felt as she walked toward the tiny restaurant was the warm caress of Ben's eyes on her back.

* * *

The Glendale was elegant and expensive. Maria was glad she'd had a chance to return to her apartment and dress with care. She only owned one cocktail dress, but the red silk sheath with thin straps suited her perfectly. The color was dramatic, but with her hair done up in a loose twist on the top of her head and a simple pair of small gold hoops in her ears, the effect was understated and stylish.

Since it was a week night, the restaurant wasn't busy, and the service was so excellent they were finished with their meal before nine o'clock.

Maria looked at her watch. "Linda won't even be closing the restaurant for another half an hour," she said. "I guess I could call it an early evening."

Ben picked up his wineglass and took a sip. "Or I guess we could go upstairs and have a cup of coffee." He sat his glass down carefully. "It might be more comfortable." His eyes held hers, the challenge they'd issued all day still subtly visible.

Maria didn't look away, but her mouth felt dry. "It might be more comfortable, but I'm not sure it would be...wise."

"As wise as we want it to be. I'd let you decide."

Maria sighed. "I was afraid of that."

Ben raised a finger to signal for their check, his eyes asking for permission. She nodded, the slightest incline of her head, and Ben finished the motion that brought the waiter instantly to their table.

They left the restaurant, and as they crossed the brightly lit lobby of the hotel, Maria felt pride at seeing their reflections in the mirrored hallway next to the bank of elevators. Ben looked incredibly attractive in his dark suit, and her red dress complemented him like a rosebud in his lapel.

Ben took her hand as they rode up in the elevator and he held it even as he unlocked his door and flipped on the light.

He used his hold on her hand to tug her into his arms as the door swung shut behind them. Maria didn't resist. She'd been heading toward his arms since dawn.

His hands brushed along the length of her back, over the smooth roundness of her shoulders, grasping her upper arms to keep her pressed close. But his kiss was not the rough, lawless passion of the night of the storm. It explored—learning her taste and feel and exquisite textures. She was willing to give him all the time he needed to learn all he cared to know. She leaned her head back, arching against him to expose the length of her neck, her earlobes, her collarbone, the hollow at the base of her throat, all available to his questing mouth.

His lips left her skin and she opened her eyes to find him smiling down at her. She couldn't help but smile in return.

His smile turned into a chuckle. "I keep expecting one of the kids to come running in," he said. "I've got an ear half-cocked, listening for them."

Maria nodded. "I know what you mean."

He guided her to the couch that faced floor-to-ceiling windows and pulled her down next to him. He enfolded her against his chest, wrapping his arms around her while they looked out at the lights of the city below them. He nuzzled her hair with his chin, loosening the pins that held it up until the heavy mass fell to her shoulders.

"I can't believe how much I like having all of you at my house," he said as he relaxed against the cushions. "How did Vergie and I manage, rattling around in that big old house, just the two of us?"

Maria leaned her head back to rest against the breadth of his chest. "It's a wonderful summer for the children. They're going to remember it for the rest of their lives."

"So am I," Ben said.

She twisted her head to look up at him, to judge his seriousness by his eyes, and he took advantage of the movement to claim her lips again. But the quality of his caresses reflected a passion kept in tight control, a fire carefully banked. Their first venture toward physical intimacy had left them both bruised and Maria knew he sensed her inner wariness in spite of the way her body responded to him.

"I take it we're going to be very wise tonight," he said, smoothing her hair back from her face, tucking a strand behind her ear with a gentle finger.

"Very," she agreed. "Is that all right?" She searched his face for signs of disappointment but saw only understanding.

"I guess it will have to be. I'm a patient man and you are a very cautious woman."

"I—"

"Don't apologize." He laid a finger across her lips. "You have every reason to be cautious." Then he replaced his finger with his lips and proceeded to kiss her in a way that wasn't the least bit cautious.

And his kisses broke through to some place in her soul that she'd barricaded behind suspicion and cynicism since she was nine years old. Maria fell in love with Ben Calder and it didn't matter if he was a "good" man or a "bad" man or "just" a man. All that mattered was that he was Ben Calder, the man she loved. And she accepted all the good and all the bad and reveled in the joy of the whole.

It was well past midnight when Ben drove up to her apartment. And it was several more long minutes before she made her way, slightly dazed, up the stairs and through her front door where she completely forgot to ask Linda how her evening at the restaurant had gone.

* * *

"I take it you had a good time in Phoenix." Maria's mother looked at her closely as the women sat on the porch after supper the next night. Ben and Maria had arrived back at the ranch just in time for Mrs. Romero's famous chicken tacos and then had parted company to shower after the long drive. Maria sat in her usual place on the steps, rubbing her damp hair with a towel, a cup of coffee at her feet.

"I had a very good time." She ignored her mother's probing eyes. "The restaurant had one of the best June's ever and Linda looks good. She sends her love."

"Aunt Linda sends you kisses, little sweet." Veronica lifted Ashley above her head and grinned up at her. Everyone seemed happy that evening; the children played tag on the lawn, and Connor had told jokes nonstop at the supper table until they'd been almost in tears with laughter. The fact that Maria had returned from Phoenix positively glowing had lightened everyone's spirits.

Maria watched the main house expectantly. Ben hadn't said anything, but she knew he would join her tonight on the porch for the first time in more than a week. And she would welcome him. She would see where their relationship led. She knew she was opening herself up to the possibility of being hurt; she faced that possibility head on and she accepted it. She wanted to take the risk. There was a good chance he would never love her back, or that he would love her and leave, anyway. There were a million ways he could disappoint her, hurt her, abandon her—and none of them mattered. She didn't care anymore. She was willing to risk each of those million ways to see him striding toward her the way he was right now, his own hair curling damply around his ears, his own eyes just as willing.

Ben smiled down at her. Maria moved her coffee cup to the other side of her feet and waited for him to sit beside her.

She didn't shift when his shoulder pressed against hers; in fact, she leaned toward him, luxuriating in his strength.

"Ben!" Tina broke away from the group of children and ran up. She threw her arms around him and kissed him on the cheek. "I'm so glad you came. I hated it when you stopped coming to the porch. I couldn't even go to sleep that way."

Ben returned the child's hug and looked at Maria over the head of her youngest daughter, a glance full of tenderness for both mother and child.

Tina snuggled onto his lap. "You don't mind that I asked Ben to come sit on the porch with us tonight, do you, Mama?"

"You asked Ben to come?" Maria was surprised.

Tina nodded. "I asked him after dinner. I missed him so much. I love him, Mama." Tina's small voice was high and clear and honest and so open—love as only a child can give it, given with her entire being.

Maria felt stark fear course through her, clenching her stomach, tightening her lungs, her throat, until she could barely draw breath. That openness she saw in her daughter's face, a complete faith in her love with no concept of the idea that anyone could ever hurt her, forced every trace of color from Maria's face.

Maria stared up at Ben, eyes huge, trying to squeeze the words past her paralyzed throat. "I quit," she whispered. "I quit."

Chapter Eight

Panic gripped Maria so tightly she didn't notice the way Ben's face had also paled at Tina's words, the way his every muscle had tensed.

When he spoke, his voice was controlled, devoid of emotion. "You can't quit. The day after tomorrow I've got to move five hundred head of cattle thirty miles. I'll have six extra men to feed. I need a cook."

"I'm sorry. I have to go. I—" Didn't he understand? She *had* to go—for her daughters' sake. She'd been willing to take the risk, prepared for the consequences, but she'd totally forgotten that she would be forcing her daughters to take the same risk and live with the same consequences. She remembered only too well what the consequences could be. She would not subject her girls to the pain, the confusion, the desperate suffering that she'd had to live through when her father had left her.

They had been young enough that Marcus's death hadn't affected them; they knew their father only through her stories. But they would remember Ben. And when Ben left, when he walked away from his responsibilities, when he acted like all the men of her experience did, they would suffer. Their pain would add to Maria's own pain a thousandfold; their pain would be unbearable for her in a way her own would not be.

A part of her knew her reaction was irrational, extreme—a part of her tried to shout it wasn't fair to expect so little from Ben, or to place the burden of other men's blame on him. But the maternal instinct to protect her children was louder, stronger, and the only voice she could hear.

"I'm sorry," she repeated helplessly. Something in Ben's eyes frightened her. They were pale gray in a face unnaturally still, chiseled from desert sandstone.

"You can leave as soon as we're through moving the cattle, but I need you until then," Ben said tonelessly. "Connor will leave then, too. After that, I can manage on my own until Vergie gets back in August."

"All right." Maria nodded.

"What is it, Mama?" Tina looked at the adults in confusion. "We're not going anywhere, are we?"

"Not right now, love," Maria told her. "We're going to stay here for a whole week more."

"That's a long time?"

"A very long time." Maria lifted the child from Ben's lap and held her close. It was a protective gesture, an unconscious movement to put distance between Ben and her family, to begin building the wall of separation.

Ben stood and looked past Maria as he spoke. "I've got paperwork to finish up tonight. I better get started on it." He walked away from them stiffly, as if aware of the rotation of his joints, as if the movement were painful to him.

"Do you want to explain that?" Veronica asked, her voice tight and angry.

"No."

"Maria—"

"I don't want to talk about it." Maria picked up Tina and
carried her up the steps and into the house, unwilling to let
go.

The cabin and outbuildings were barely visible among the
aspens and pines. Their unpeeled logs seemed a part of the
still-living trees. Only a small area had been cleared around
the front of the cabin, and the trees and undergrowth
pressed close along the back and sides, ready to reclaim it in
only a season or two.

Maria was glad to get out of the truck, the long ride with
Ben and Connor had been excruciating. Even Ben's glow-
ering after their fight last week was preferable to the icy
calm, the frozen reserve, he'd shown her for the past two
days. She was thankful to see Harvey, with his gap-toothed
smile, amble toward them from one of the smaller log cabins. He and the hired men had come up the day before,
pulling the cumbersome horse trailers behind their trucks.

"You remember to bring the fireworks?" Harvey asked
Connor. He lowered the tailgate and began to unload the
truck, lifting out a box filled with canned goods.

"I've got them." Connor tucked a sack under each arm
and started for the cabin.

"Good enough. Too bad there wasn't enough room for
the kiddies to come stay up here with you, Maria. They
would have got a kick out of the Fourth of July we put on."

"They would have loved it," Maria said, looking around
her at the nature-ready playground. She would have pre-
ferred to have the children there as well to provide a noisy
buffer between herself and Ben. Harvey and the men would
take meals with them, but otherwise they would stay in the
nearby bunkhouse. She dreaded the long evenings of forced

isolation with Ben. Connor would be no help in filling the interminable hours; he was an expert at withdrawing into himself and would never even consider making polite conversation.

She grabbed the strings of a navy blue sleeping bag, pulled it to her and cradled its down bulk to her chest as she made her way inside. The cabin consisted of one large room and a loft reached by means of a steep set of stairs that were more ladder than stairs. A set of bunk beds was pushed against the back wall, an old leather couch and bookshelf lined a side wall, while a huge butcher block table took up the majority of the room with backless benches that ran its length. Kerosene lanterns hung from hooks on the ceiling. The kitchen consisted of a set of cupboards, a refrigerator with rounded corners, a chipped white sink with a sparse foot of counter space and a squat, black monstrosity that cowered in the corner and caused Maria to let out a gasp of dismay.

Maria's curses could be heard clear out to the truck. Since they were in Spanish they couldn't be literally translated, but the emotion behind them was easily understood.

"I take it you didn't tell her about Black Beauty?" Harvey grunted as he hoisted another box. Ben shook his head.

Connor grinned. He nudged his father in the back with the box he held in his arms. "After you, Dad."

Harvey moved behind Connor and they both waited for Ben to lead the way. Ben opened the screen door with his foot and ducked the sleeping bag that flew at him.

"*¡Madre de Dios!*" Maria shouted, twirling around to face him. "That—that thing better not be what I think it is!"

"It's a wood-burning stove," Ben said calmly.

"I'm supposed to cook on it! I'm supposed to cook three meals a day for ten people on a wood stove? You've got to be kidding me!"

"I told you the cabin didn't have electricity."

"But you said there was a propane tank to run the refrigerator. I thought you'd have a propane stove, too."

"Nope, only Black Beauty there." Ben sat his box down on the table and surveyed the cast-iron stove.

"She's been in the family since 1912," Harvey told her with pride. "She makes the best pancakes you've ever tasted."

"There's no running water, either," Connor added happily. "You have to carry it in from the spring outside in those buckets."

"No, *you* have to carry it in for me," Maria told him, hands on her hips.

"Did you know there's an outhouse?" Connor shot over his shoulder, ducking out the door as if fearful another sleeping bag would be coming his way.

Maria refused to look at Ben, afraid that his cool stare would be her undoing. Instead, she stalked after the boy to the truck for another load.

By the time they had the supplies unloaded and put away it was evening and time to start supper. Ben gave her a perfunctory cooking lesson, showed her how large a fire to build, which sections of the stove were hotter than others and lifted down the huge cast-iron skillets from hooks on the wall. It was accomplished with a minimum of words and a careful distance between them.

She managed to turn out passable hamburgers, although the first batch was a little rare from lack of wood and the second batch was slightly charred from adding a few sticks too many. But with a pot of baked beans and a huge tin bowl of salad, none of the men went back to the bunk-house hungry or complaining. By the time water was heated to wash the dishes and the kitchen was back in order, Maria was so tired she no longer gave a thought to any uncomfortable silences there might be in the cabin that night. She flopped on the couch and closed her eyes, her legs stretched out in front of her.

Ben lay on his back on the top bunk at the end of the room, a book propped on his chest, one foot swinging free off the side of the bed. Connor sat at the table, staring intently at the miniature screen of a hand-held video game, his flying fingers instant death to the on-screen aliens. The occasional whisper of a page turning, the clunk of a log settling in the stove, the hiss of the kerosene lamps, were the only sounds in the cabin.

Maria heard Connor shift at the table and rummage through his backpack. She opened her eyes a crack and was amazed to see him pull out a sketchbook and flip it open. He looked at his father out of the corner of his eye, but Ben seemed intent on his book.

Connor began to draw. Every few minutes he would tear a sheet from the pad and lay it on the table in front of him. He made a show of tearing out the paper, a slow, loud rip plainly heard throughout the room. Soon, the table around him was covered with drawings. Maria watched him through half-open eyes, wondering at his purpose. He seemed to be making thumbnail sketches of items in the room. He'd study an object for a moment, his pencil would fly across the paper, then he'd tear out the page and add it to the pile on the table. All the while keeping an eye on his father.

Connor's strange behavior made Maria restless and she began to sit up.

"Hold still," Connor barked. "I'm doing you."

Maria sank back down, motionless, until a few seconds later Connor flicked his wrist and added her picture to the stack. "Okay, all done."

That finally caught Ben's attention. He looked up. "What are you doing?"

"Drawing."

"Uhmm." Ben nodded noncommittally and returned to his book.

Maria couldn't believe it. Ben didn't seem aware that Connor's little drama was being enacted on his behalf. She caught Connor's eye and was shocked to see the purpose there. He'd obviously come to some kind of decision and was determined to see it through.

"Would you like to take a look?" Connor refused to let the matter drop.

"Sure." Ben seemed surprised by the offer. He dropped down from the bunk bed and went to stand beside his son. He stood quite still for a very long time. Neither Connor nor Maria broke the silence as they watched him stare down at the papers on the table. Ben reached out a hand and slid some of the sheets over so he could see the ones beneath. He picked one up and studied it more closely.

Without a word, he carried the paper over and handed it to Maria. It was the sketch Connor had just completed of her. With no more than half a dozen strokes of the pencil, Connor had captured her slumped posture, the tired tilt of her head, the weary lines of her body as she'd sat on the couch. Ben looked at her, a question in his eyes, as if seeking confirmation of what he thought he saw. She nodded, a silent assurance that, indeed, here was an amazing talent, and handed the drawing back to him.

Ben cleared his throat. "How long have you been drawing like this?"

Connor shrugged. "Three or four years, I guess."

"Why haven't you ever shown me this before?"

"Why haven't you ever looked before?"

Ben's chin shot up and he started to speak, but then he closed his mouth, obviously biting back an angry retort. "You know how good you are?" he asked instead.

"Yes."

"What are you doing about it?"

"My art teacher arranged for me to take a night class at the university last semester and I'm going to take another one this fall. He says there's no art classes left at the high school that would do me any good."

Ben nodded. "You know," he said, his voice thoughtful, "winters are long on the ranch and it's good to have another interest. When you take over Calder Ranch, you'll need to keep up with your art. A gift like this shouldn't be wasted."

"I'm not taking over Calder Ranch, Dad. I've told you that before." Connor sounded calm and composed without his usual petulance.

"I know, but you're still young yet." Ben held up his hand to stop Connor's immediate objections. "I don't mean to dismiss the way you feel right now. I really do understand what you're saying. But Calder Ranch is in your blood, and I think in a few years you'll see that this is where you belong."

"The ranch is where *you* belong, not me!" Connor jumped to his feet, so agitated he tipped over the bench. "It's in *your* blood, in *your* water, in *your* air. To me it's just a miserable, dusty chunk of desert full of stinking animals and I don't want it!" His adult composure had left him, exposing the trembling child within. "I'm going to art college. I'm going to be an artist, not a rancher. Mom called me. She told me you went to see her when you were in Phoenix and that you told her you want me to start spending all summer up here with you. Well, no way!'' Connor shouted. "Do you hear me? No way!''

Connor's eyes darted around the cabin like a cornered rabbit looking for an escape. But the one-room cabin had nowhere to bolt to, no separate room to disappear into behind a slammed door. Instead, he threw himself onto the bottom bunk and zipped himself into his sleeping bag, his back turned to the room, shutting them out.

Ben remained by the table, his eyes on the strewn papers. Slowly, he folded the picture of Maria he still held in his hands, carefully creasing the paper. He took out his wallet, laid the paper inside and returned the wallet to the back pocket of his jeans. He stood for a long moment, then straightened his shoulders and walked out the heavy log door of the cabin, disappearing into the night.

Maria desperately wanted to follow him. She wanted to wrap her arms around him and cradle his head to her shoulder, comfort him, stand with him in the darkness and offer him whatever strength she had to give. But she knew she dared not. She knew that anything she did that drew her closer to Ben would only prolong the agony, would only make her departure that much more unbearable, would only cause her more pain. She would be leaving him soon, very soon. She had to leave. It was the right thing to do, the only thing. The sooner she got used to the idea, the better.

So instead of following Ben as every instinct screamed for her to do, Maria practiced leaving. One by one, she turned the knobs on the kerosene lanterns until they gave only the faintest glow. Then she climbed the ladder to the loft, undressed and slid into her sleeping bag, where she lay awake and listened for the sound of Ben's return.

Ben shuddered as icy water cascaded over his head and dripped down his bare chest and shoulders. He scooped another handful from the spring and splashed it on his face, doing it again and again until his eyes didn't feel so full of grit and his brain so sluggish. It was always hard to get a good night's sleep the first night on the mountain, what with the added altitude, the hard bunk, the strange surroundings. But last night it had been almost impossible. He'd heard Connor toss and turn into the small hours of the morning, and Maria had obviously been awake, as well.

That fact added to Ben's wakefulness more than any of the others. Picturing her so near, lying in the loft, able to hear her body shift on the old mattress that covered the ancient brass bed, to hear her occasional soft sigh—all had combined to make sleep out of the question. He had tortured himself with memories of Maria in his arms—the night of the movie, during the flash flood, in his hotel in Phoenix. He'd seen her in his garden, his kitchen, the cherry tree, the porch steps, sitting across from him in an elegant restaurant wearing a flame-colored dress that set him on fire. Every memory made him twist and turn and curse the confines of a sleeping bag that wasn't quite long enough for his frame.

He shook the water out of his eyes and reached for his shirt. He buttoned it over his still-damp chest, tucked it into his jeans, and turned up the cuffs with quick, efficient movements as he surveyed his mountain property. The horses grazed docilely in the small corral while smoke curled from the chimney of the bunkhouse, a sign that the men were up and getting ready for the day. The door to the outhouse banged occasionally, sending startled birds into the sky and chipmunks racing along pine branches.

Ben ran his fingers through his hair, smoothed it down and headed back for the cabin. He found Maria already up and the table covered with bread, cheese, meats and all the makings for sandwiches. She had a finished stack of sand viches wrapped in plastic and sitting in a box, along with apples, candy bars, cans of nuts and tuna—all high-energy food ready to be stuffed into saddlebags to feed the men throughout the day since they wouldn't return to the cabins until evening.

Ben opened the heavy black door of the stove and squatted on his heels in front of it. He stirred the coals with a poker, added kindling and carefully breathed life back into the embers. When the fire was burning briskly, he fitted the door shut and made himself a cup of instant coffee with the lukewarm water that had simmered all night in the teakettle.

He watched Maria while she spread butter on bread, assembly-line style. The dark smudges under her brown eyes made her appear even more fragile than usual. In contrast to the rough-hewn logs of the cabin, the curtainless windows, the yellowed vinyl on the floor, she appeared utterly feminine, even in jeans, tennis shoes and a gray hooded sweatshirt. He tore his eyes from her; he had no time to stand around daydreaming. He drained his cup in one swallow, sat it in the sink and went to wake up Connor.

The boy lay on his back with the sleeping bag pushed down to his waist. One arm was outflung, fingers almost brushing the floor. Ben reached out a hand to shake his shoulder, but paused. Instead, his hand went to Connor's forehead and brushed back his hair, smoothed it off his face, a face young and childlike in sleep.

Ben remembered the way Connor always used to be the first one in the cabin awake, as excited to start moving the cattle as if it were Christmas morning. He would dash outside and gallop through the long, wet grass, following the men around and getting in their way until his pant legs were soaked with dew and he was sent inside to change. His horse was always in front, next to Ben's, and he'd gamely keep up until well into the afternoon. When his head would start to nod, Ben would gather him onto his horse, tuck the boy in front of him and wrap an arm around him, holding his drooping, sweaty little body close while they ambled along ahead of the herd.

Ben's mouth softened but the gentle smile faded as he saw Connor's eyelids flicker. He dreaded the moment when Connor's eyes would open and he would see the antagonism there, the antipathy reserved for Ben alone. He didn't use to look at him like that.

Ben thought of little Tina, how she'd stared up at him with such open adoration when she'd said she loved him that evening on the porch. He clamped down hard on the memory. He refused to think about it. The girls and their mother would be on their way back to Phoenix in a few short days. That was best, for them and for him.

"Time to get up." Ben's voice was gruff as he touched Connor's shoulder. "I want you to help Harvey get the horses saddled before breakfast."

Connor mumbled a response and groped for the sleeping bag, but Ben stripped it down to his feet before the boy's searching hand could grasp it. "Now," he ordered.

"All right, already," Connor snapped, struggling to sit up. He glared at his father with swollen eyes.

Ben straightened and turned to see Maria standing next to the sink with a loaf of bread in her hand, looking bewildered. The sandwiches were finished and the table cleared.

"What's the matter?"

"Toast," Maria said with a frown. "How do you make toast without a toaster?"

She looked so serious, so worried, Ben wanted nothing more than to gather her into his arms. But instead of crushing her to him and kissing her until she didn't give a damn about toast, he calmly opened a cupboard and lifted out a

rack. He showed her how it fit into a special slot inside the
stove where the bread would gently toast over the hot
coals—or burn to a crisp black curl if you left it in a second
too long.

"I'll do the first batch so you can see how it's done," Ben
volunteered.

Maria thanked him politely and began to lay strips of bacon in one skillet and crack eggs in another. Ben buttered
bread and placed the slices on the rack, then shoved the rack
into the stove, keeping a careful eye on it while he stacked a
pile of plates on one end of the table and threw a jumble of
silverware next to it. The men began to straggle in. Each
grabbed a plate and took it to the stove where Maria ladled
eggs, bacon, hash browns and toast onto it, then they sat
themselves on one of the benches, wolfed down their food
in a minimum of bites and lined up for seconds.

Maria never left the stove, empty egg cartons piled up on
the counter and bacon sizzled nonstop. It took her only a
few tries before the toast came out of the oven golden
brown. Ben watched her wield the spatula, dwarfed by the
mammoth stove, her hands so delicate they didn't look
strong enough to manhandle the enormous skillets. Yet she
turned out a mountain of food with little fuss. She had a
smudge of soot on the front of her sweatshirt from brushing against the door of the oven and tendrils of hair came
loose from her braid. Her nose was shiny from the heat and
she looked so lovely that Ben ached.

He stood, the signal it was time to start. The men gulped
the last of their coffee, grabbed their hats and left the
kitchen en masse. They left behind stacks of dishes, crumpled paper napkins and the smell of horses, cigarettes and
bacon.

Harvey and Connor had the horses saddled and waiting,
but each man checked his saddle himself, tightening the

cinch to his own personal preference. The horses were eager to start and nickered to one another, stomping and
blowing into the cool early-morning air. Ben felt the same
anticipation. Rounding up the cattle and moving them to
new pasture would take four full days and long hours in the
saddle, but the recalcitrant cows, the sore muscles, the dust,
the camaraderie with the men, they were all things Ben
wouldn't miss for the world.

Maria stood at the door to the cabin and watched them
mount, wiping her hands on a checkered cloth. Ben rode
over to her and looked down from the added height of
horseback. He felt the urge to say something, to thank her,
to kiss her, to— Hell, he didn't know what he wanted to do.
Instead, he tipped his hat to her and swung his horse
around. With a flick of the reins he started away from the
cabin at a trot while his men fell into place behind him.
Feeling like some ridiculous second-rate actor in a western
movie, he followed the trail into the trees until the cabin and
Maria disappeared from sight.

Maria pushed aside a dirty plate and made a space for
herself on one end of the table to eat her own breakfast.
While she ate the last of the eggs in the skillet and nibbled
on a strip of bacon, she thought about supper for the men.
The roast she'd planned was out. In spite of Harvey's as-
surances that the little space beside the stove was a perfect
oven, capable of turning out golden cakes and fluffy biscuits, she wasn't about to chance it. She refused to cook a
roast in an oven without a temperature gauge. Everything
would either have to be fried, boiled or anything else you
could do on top of a stove, for the remainder of the time in
the cabin.

She decided the roast would do well enough as a pot roast
and sat about peeling potatoes, carrots and onions. She

rought out a Dutch oven, laid in the meat and sprinkled it
ith salt and pepper. Then she added the vegetables and
ome water and sat the pan on the back of the stove to sim-
er. At eight thousand feet above sea level it would take
ours to cook.

Supper taken care of, Maria heated water and tackled the
reakfast dishes. Then she straightened the cabin and re-
lled the wood bin next to the stove from the pile of split
gs beside the cabin. She heated another pan of water and
ad a more thorough bath than she'd been able to take with
e men present, and changed into shorts and a clean blouse.
eeling refreshed, Maria left the cabin and stood outside in
e warm sunshine. She hadn't given much thought to the
ct that she'd be easily finished with her chores by noon
nd, since the men wouldn't return until close to dark, she'd
ave a long afternoon to herself.

Normally the prospect of several hours alone, without the
ildren's demands or a stack of work, would have de-
ghted her, but now the unaccustomed silence and solitude
ade her edgy. She spied the path Ben and the horses had
ken on the other side of the clearing and decided to walk
r a while. The path followed a small stream that chased
ver rocks and under fallen trees and waited for her to catch
p in quiet little pools of shade. Maria enjoyed the exercise
d the beauty around her, but she had hoped they would
ccupy her mind as well as her body. Instead, they tended
 focus her thoughts even more sharply on things she didn't
ant to dwell on, most particularly on the look in Ben's eyes
at morning before he'd ridden away.

The indifference had been gone as he'd looked down at
er from his horse. His eyes had blazed at her, gray smoke
aring her, full of meaning. And yet their meaning had left
laria confused and uncertain. She turned and retraced her

steps, no longer noticing the shadowy pine trees or the tiny wildflowers, no longer hearing the cheerful stream.

Maria went inside the cabin and paced about restlessly for a while. Disconsolate, she climbed onto Ben's bunk and laid down on top of his sleeping bag. She hugged his pillow to her chest and buried her nose in it, savoring his masculine scent that lingered there. In only a few moments she was asleep, worn out from lack of sleep the night before.

She awoke to find Ben leaning over her, his face near hers. Late-afternoon light filtered into the cabin and the delicious aroma of roast filled the air.

"Have you seen Connor?" Ben asked, evidently repeating himself. "Has he been back to the cabin?"

"What's that matter?" Groggily, she propped herself up on an elbow. "I thought you weren't coming back until dark."

"Nothing's the matter." But the look in his eyes contradicted his words. "Have you seen Connor?"

Maria shook her head. She pushed her hair out of her eyes and sat up. "What is it?"

Ben's face twisted with worry. "Connor's missing."

Chapter Nine

"Nobody's seen him since lunchtime." Ben didn't waste
[ti]me on further explanation. He was already heading out the
[d]oor. "If I'm not back with Connor by the time the men
[c]ome in tonight, tell them he's still missing and send them
[o]ut to search the north slope of the mesa. There's a full
[m]oon tonight, we should be able to see well enough." The
[d]oor slammed behind him and by the time Maria managed
[t]o jump down from the bunk and run after him, his horse
[h]ad disappeared into the trees.

When the men came back to the cabin shortly before
[d]ark, there was no sign of either Ben or Connor. Maria re-
[la]yed Ben's instructions to Harvey who immediately took
[ch]arge, supervising the feeding and care of the weary horses
[an]d saddling the fresh horses that waited in the corral.

She had to beg the men to have something to eat before
[th]ey rode out again. Her tender pot roast might as well have
[be]en shoe leather for all the attention the worried group at
[th]e table gave it. They were on their feet and had picked up

their hats while still chewing their last mouthful. She had a
half-dozen thermoses full of hot coffee ready and waiting
for them to take as they left. But she could do no more than
watch while the men got stiffly back into the saddle, urged
their horses to a trot and, armed with flashlights, set out into
the rapidly fading twilight.

It was close to two in the morning when she heard foot
steps and subdued voices outside. She lay in the loft and
listened to the sound of the men returning. The cabin door
opened and the tap of Ben's boots echoed hollowly in the
early-morning quiet. He didn't light a lamp, and Maria
heard the couch springs squeak as he lowered himself onto
it.

"Ben?" she asked softly

"Yeah. It's me."

"Connor?"

"No sign of him." Ben's voice was low and controlled.

Maria knew there was nothing more to say. She stared
into the dark. No sound of movement came from below,
only Ben's breathing, which grew heavier, deep and even.
She climbed downstairs and found Ben still sitting on the
couch, head tilted back, fully dressed and sound asleep. She
dragged the sleeping bag off his bunk and laid it over him.
Unable to resist, she kissed him softly on the cheek before
climbing to the loft again.

Ben and the men rode off the next morning as soon as
was light. They'd bolted down their breakfast, studied the
maps Ben had spread out on the floor, then left to search
their assigned areas. They were a subdued, serious group of
men who knew only too well the dangers of the mountain
and the elements, fully aware that every passing minute
multiplied the danger to Connor.

By the time the sun finally dragged itself over the moun
tains and sent a few golden shafts to dry the dew on the ta

ass, Maria was alone, with little to do but wait and worry.
he grew almost fond of the squat black stove as the day
ore on, feeding it wood gave her something to do and
lped mark off the hours. Its warmth was welcome by late
ternoon as the sky began to cloud over. The cabin felt chill
d damp—the weak gray light coming through the win-
ws didn't penetrate to the corners of the room—and she
the kerosene lamps early to help dispel the gloom.

A steady drizzle misted the mountains by the time the
archers returned, cold and exhausted, unable to continue
th the moon's light obscured by the clouds. Maria didn't
ed to ask if they'd found Connor. Their tight faces told
r everything. They ate the steaks Maria had pan fried and
aggled to the bunkhouse to get some sleep and prepare for
other day's search in the morning.

Harvey was the last to leave. "I listened to the radio in the
ck," he told them. "Weather report said this storm
ould move off around midnight and be clear as a bell to-
orrow."

"That's good," Ben said.

"Yup." Harvey nodded. He paused next to the door and
eaded his beat-up brown hat in his hands. Maria saw him
arch for words, for the right thing to say. "Well, good
ght, boss," he finally said, giving up. There weren't any
hts words, Maria knew.

"'Night, Harvey." Ben stared at the closed door for sev-
al minutes, then he pushed himself up from the table and
lked over to the bookcase. He pulled a canvas cover off
ig square box that sat on the top shelf, revealing a two-
y radio. After fiddling with several knobs, Ben picked up
microphone and used his thumb to push in a button on
side.

"Wyberg Search and Rescue, this is Calder Mountain
se, come in, please."

"This is Wyberg. What's up, Ben?" Maria recognize
Stella McClaskey's voice even distorted by the radio.

"I've got a man missing, Stella. Can you get a team t
gether and come up to Purdy Mesa tomorrow morning?"

"We'll be there." Stella sounded confident and n
nonsense. "Horseback search?"

"And on foot, it's pretty rugged. You might be able to u
a four-wheel drive in a few places on top."

"Copy. Do you want me to notify any family dov
here?" she asked.

"That won't be necessary. It's Connor."

There was only the slight hum of static for several se
onds. "Copy." Stella's voice sounded shaky. "I'll be pra
ing, Ben. Wyberg out."

"Thanks, Stella. Calder Mountain Base out." Ben r
placed the microphone but remained standing in front of t
bookcase, his eyes blank. Maria reached out a hand to tou
his arm and was dismayed to feel how damp his shirt was

"Ben, you've got to get out of those wet clothes." But
didn't seem to hear her, his eyes still fixed on some inn
scene.

"Ben!" Maria gave his arm a shake and was reliev
when he turned his head and focused on her. "You need
change into dry clothes." She half led him to his duffel b
at the foot of the bunk bed. "You get dressed and I'll ma
us some fresh coffee, and I'll build up that fire to warm y
up."

Maria could hear the rustle of Ben's clothes as they hit t
floor while she worked in the kitchen. By the time she h
the stove roaring and the coffee made, Ben sat on the cou
in a fresh shirt and jeans. She brought over two mugs
coffee and a bottle of whiskey she'd found in the cupboa
and sat down beside him.

Rain tapped on the metal roof as they sipped the whiskey-laced coffee. Maria's shoulder touched Ben's, but it was touch of comfort, the reassurance of another human presence.

"The search-and-rescue people probably have a lot of experience finding lost people," Maria said after several minutes had passed.

"If he's lost," Ben replied cryptically.

"What do you mean?"

"Connor's spent every summer of his life in these mountains. He knows the whole area like the back of his hand. He could find his way to the cabin blindfolded, unless . . ."

"Oh, no. You think he's hurt?"

Ben shifted uneasily. "Could be his horse threw him— Belle can be cranky—or maybe a snake bite, or a fall. Hell, I don't know. Something's keeping him from coming home." Ben ran an agitated hand through his damp hair. "But even if he's hurt, he's got his .22, a good hunting knife, a canteen, rain slicker. He's got enough gear in his saddlebags to get him by for three or four days—if Belle stayed with him. But if she didn't, why hasn't she made her way back to the corral by now? Why—"

"Ben, stop it." Maria felt tension cord the muscles of his shoulder pressed against hers. "You're just making yourself crazy."

"I feel crazy," Ben muttered. He sprang up, refilled his coffee cup at the stove, then strode back to stand in front of her. "You want to know the really crazy thing?" His posture, as he looked down on her, showed a tightly reigned wildness. "Connor's been lost for the past six years—and I didn't even know it."

Ben started to pace, his nervous energy making the cabin seem even smaller and more confined. "He's got this incredible talent, and I never knew it—never noticed! Now that's crazy. How could I not have known that about my son?'' he demanded. "About my own child?"

He threw himself down next to Maria. "My son," he repeated in a brooding tone, his eyes fixed on the floor between his boots. "*My* son."

His laugh was self-berating and it frightened Maria. She cradled her mug between her hands and stared into it depths. The warm coffee reflected the lantern above their heads, a brilliant yellow orb shimmering hypnotically on top of the dark liquid. She kept silent, and when Ben finally began to talk again she couldn't be sure he even remembered she was in the room.

"He might be my son, but, by God, he sounds just like Lori sometimes. She couldn't stand the ranch, and she really disliked this cabin, and that stove—Lori *hated* that stove." He shook his head at the memory of his ex-wife. "But, all in all, Lori's a good person, and she's certainly good mother. She lives for Connor."

Ben turned to look at Maria. "Have I told you about Lori?"

"Not very much."

"Well, Lori didn't belong in Wyberg," he said emphatically, "that's for sure. She was born and raised there, but all she ever wanted was to go to the city. Any city, even Phoenix would do. I thought she'd gotten all that out of her system when we got married—she knew I would never leave the ranch. And when she had Connor, I thought..." Ben shrugged. "She stuck it out for over ten years. I have to give her credit for trying. But when she turned thirty, that was it. She said she couldn't stand it anymore, said being marooned out here in the wastelands was turning her creativity to dust. She was a dancer, you know."

"Mmm." Maria tried to be nonintrusive, not wanting to stop the cathartic flow of Ben's words.

"She's got a dance studio in Phoenix now, teaches ballet and tap to little rich girls. She's quite successful, too." Ben paused and frowned. "I don't think she consciously tries to turn Connor against the ranch, I really don't. But the way he hated the place, it's got to rub off on him, even without her meaning it to. She spoils him rotten, with the best of intentions, but I just keep thinking, 'That's not the way I would do it,' or 'I'd make sure he did this or that.'" Ben gave the same hard, mirthless laugh. "But what right do I have to say anything when I see him forty-seven days out of the year?"

Ben got up and added wood to the stove. One by one, he extinguished the lanterns, leaving only the small one in the kitchen lit. Its flickering flame cast distorting shadows around the cabin that leaped and danced on their own. He picked up a sleeping bag and brought it to the couch to lay across their laps, and Maria snuggled gratefully into its downy warmth. Ben drained his cup and refilled it straight from the whiskey bottle on the floor by their feet. The tension that had fired him seemed to dim along with the lowering lights. He sighed, tucking the cover tightly around her.

"He's slipping away, Maria," he said. "We're more like nodding acquaintances than father and son. And it's my fault."

"Now, Ben—" Maria started to interrupt, but Ben would have none of it.

"It's my fault," he insisted. "It was my place to keep our relationship intact, not Connor's. He was only eleven years old when Lori and I divorced—just a little, little boy. It was up to me to make sure we stayed as close as we were then, that he kept on loving the ranch as much as he did then." Ben smiled reminiscently. "He did love the ranch. Did I ever tell you about the time he decided to teach his pony to swim in the pond?"

Maria shook her head, smiling along with him. She lis
tened to Ben's story, to his voice as he told her more storie
about Connor's childhood, about the happy times they'
spent together. Ben chuckled out loud as he described som
of Connor's antics and Maria encouraged the memories
wanting to keep his mind from dwelling on dark thoughts
But, in spite of her best efforts, the conversation came ful
circle.

"So the fault's mine, no doubt about it," Ben con
cluded. "I messed up royal." And then, as if there was a
obvious connection between the thoughts, he added, "
know why you quit, and you're absolutely right."

Maria jerked in surprise and her foot knocked over th
whiskey bottle on the floor. She leaned over, fumbling wit
the weight of the sleeping bag on her lap, and sat the bottl
upright. She felt as if the wind had been knocked out of he

"Tina scared the hell out of me the other day," Ben ad
mitted. "I don't blame you a bit for wanting to take her an
Trisha and run back to Phoenix. After you've seen the me
I've made of Connor, I can understand there's no way you'
want me around the girls. I can't expect you to trust me t
do any better with them."

"No," Maria protested. "It's not like that at all."

"It's okay. I understand."

"But—"

Ben put a gentle finger on her lips. "It's all right. It's be
that you go." He leaned his head against the back of th
couch and closed his eyes. "God, I'm so tired."

Maria wanted to tell him that it wasn't his being with h
girls that she feared—that it was exactly the opposite. It w
his leaving that would destroy her children, not his pre
ence. But she remained silent. After all, she was a survivo
she came from a family of survivors, and survivors didn

waste their time on impossible, impractical, unreachable things—like love.

It was past midnight and the rain had almost stopped, only an occasional drop could be heard pinging against the roof. A soft wind breathed through the trees, whispering sleepily. Maria rested her head against Ben's shoulder and slowly fell asleep curled against him on the couch.

Ben shifted and Maria let out a moan of protest as pain shot through her neck. Slowly, she lifted her head off Ben's shoulder and tried to straighten it, massaging the crick at the back of her neck with a hand that tingled with pins and needles. She opened her eyes a crack and saw the inside of the cabin hazily revealed by the dense gray light of early morning.

"Try to get a few more minutes' sleep," Ben said softly. He stood and arranged the sleeping bag around her shoulders.

Maria looked at him leaning over her, so close. The shadow on his jaw and his tousled hair seemed so intimate, she felt herself grow warm and her heart danced oddly in her chest. "That's all right, I better get breakfast started."

She pushed aside the warm cocoon he'd made for her and fished under the couch for her shoes. Still half-asleep, she made her way to the kitchen where she poured warm water from the bucket on the stove into the sink and washed her hands and face. She let the water flush down the drain and refilled the sink for Ben. Ben splashed water on his face and ran a razor quickly over his skin, using the small mirror hung on the cupboard with a bent nail, while Maria brushed her teeth behind him. Sharing such morning rituals made her intensely aware of him, of his maleness, and she fled to the loft to change out of her wrinkled clothes while he finished getting ready and cared for the fire.

Climbing down again, feeling more awake and less gritty, she started the morning's chores. "I'll get some water." She picked up the two aluminum buckets. Getting water had been Connor's job and, by the look on Ben's face, she knew he was remembering that.

"I'll go with you." He took one of the pails from her hand. "They're heavy when they're full."

Maria followed him to the edge of the woods where a natural spring bubbled out of the ground into a tiny, pebble-lined pool. The pristine water was crystal clear, filtered through layers of the earth itself, and teeth-achingly cold. Maria handed Ben her bucket and watched while he kneeled beside the pool and let the water slowly gurgle over its rim. He was filling the second bucket when they heard a horse whinny softly and the sound of hooves on the trail nearby.

Connor came into sight, riding his mare, both horse and rider looking fit and healthy.

Ben was on his feet in an instant, the bucket forgotten in the pool. With a few long steps, he was beside his son. He practically pulled Connor from the saddle and began to run his hands over the boy. "Are you all right? Are you hurt?" He searched for signs of injury with competent intensity.

"I'm fine, Dad," Connor assured him. "I'm okay. Really."

Ben stopped his frantic inventory and enveloped Connor in hug. "Dammit, you scared us to death. Where in the hell were you!"

Ben held his son so tightly Maria wondered how Connor could breathe, let alone answer. "Well, I—"

"Wait," Ben interrupted. He pulled back from Connor but kept a hand firmly on each shoulder. He looked his son in the eye, eyes as gray as his own. "I have to tell you something." Ben spoke slowly and distinctly. "An artist is a fine thing to be—it's a fine, honorable profession and I'd be proud to have an artist for a son. Is that clear?''

Tears sprang to Connor's eyes. He nodded vigorously while he tried to blink them away, making his long bangs dance across his forehead.

''Good!'' Ben slapped Connor on the back and his smile was brighter than the rays of sun bursting over the mountain. ''Maria, run tell the men Connor's home—I've got to radio Wyberg and call off the search team. Connor, see to Belle, then fill up those water buckets. That's your job, you know.''

''Yes, sir,'' Connor said, and he moved to obey his father's orders faster and happier than Maria had ever seen before.

By the time Maria had finished a victory waltz around the bunkhouse with Harvey and made her way back to the cabin, Connor and Ben were sitting at the table with hot mugs of coffee in their hands.

Maria walked directly to the refrigerator. ''Let me get you some breakfast,'' she said, pulling out eggs, butter and a box of sausage patties. ''You must be starving.''

But Connor shook his head. ''I already had breakfast. I had some rabbit leftover from last night.''

Maria stopped, a carton of eggs balanced precariously on top of the pile in her arms, and looked at Connor. Ben was also staring at his son. ''I think you better tell us all about this—from the beginning,'' he said. ''And start with how you could get lost in these mountains.''

''I wasn't lost.''

Ben looked at Maria. ''Not lost?'' he repeated. ''And you weren't hurt?''

Connor shook his head.

''Are you saying you . . . ran away?''

"Not exactly. Not intentionally, anyway." Connor fidgeted with the sugar bowl on the table, but he kept his eyes firmly fixed on his father. His face was flushed yet there was determination there, too. "I just—well, I was sort of straggling along after lunch, clear at the back of the herd, and I just kept getting farther and farther behind. Then the cows dropped into that valley near Squatter's Creek and I sort of found myself alone up on top." He shrugged, helpless to explain the unexplainable. "Somehow, I just never bothered to catch back up again. I got off Belle and started walking, just thinking about...things, and next thing I knew it was getting dark."

Maria listened while she cooked. She whipped eggs, buttered bread for toast, fried sausage, scarcely noticing what her hands did she was so intent on Connor's story, as if she'd always cooked on a temperamental wood stove.

"So where does the 'why-I've-been-gone-for-two-nights' part come in?" The tone of Ben's voice showed that his initial jubilation and relief had faded, and parental outrage was ready to replace it.

But Connor didn't flinch. "I started to ride back to the cabin, but I was pretty hungry, and then I spied a rabbit. Well, by the time I got him skinned and cooked, it was really late, so I decided to make camp and come home the next morning. I was still pretty mad at you about...things." Connor lifted his chin. His voice was quiet and steady. "At the time, I didn't really care if you were worried or not.

"But when I got up the next morning—" Connor struggled again for words. "Dad, I pulled a trout out of Squatter's Creek with my bare hands! Remember how you taught me to do that when I was little? I laid him on the foil wrappers from a couple of candy bars and cooked him for breakfast. It was so beautiful, and so quiet, and I didn't have anything—no music or my drawing stuff, nothing—

just me and Belle. I didn't want to leave. I couldn't leave!"
He leaned forward, intense, trying to make his father understand. "I had plenty of water in my canteen, I had my rifle, all kinds of supplies, and you know how I always wanted to follow that track up to that old silver mine—"

"You didn't! How many times have I told you not—" Ben stopped himself with an obvious effort.

"I didn't go into the mine. I know how dangerous that would be. But the climb was so cool." Connor sounded triumphant. "Dad, I'd forgotten how much I used to like to camp out with you. Remember how we always used to go camping over by Mud Springs? I'd forgotten how much I really love this country. Maria—" he turned toward her "—don't you think this is the most beautiful mountain in the world?"

Maria nodded her head and laughed while she piled sausages onto a platter. She'd never heard such joy in Connor's voice before.

"That explains why we couldn't find you," Ben said. "We only looked within a day's ride of the cabin. I never gave a thought to starting out cross-country."

"I really meant to come home yesterday evening, I really meant to, but then it started to rain and Belle's foreleg seemed to be bothering her a little bit. I didn't see any sense in sloshing around in the mud and ending up with a lame horse. I had that plastic tarp in my saddlebag, so I stretched it over a branch and made camp for the night. Then I started back as soon as I could this morning."

Connor paused and drew himself up. "I know I worried you and I'm really sorry. I was having a wonderful time playing mountain man and you were all probably worried sick. I was only thinking about myself, and it was a childish, selfish thing to do."

But Maria didn't think Connor sounded childish. In fact, there was a new maturity about him. Whatever he'd thought about for the past day and a half, whatever insights he'd learned about himself, the ranch, his father, during his self-imposed solitude, had caused him to grow past the selfish child he called himself. He offered no excuses, but sat patiently, waiting for his father to pass judgment.

Ben must have seen the same changes in his son that Maria did, must have noted the way he accepted responsibility for his actions, because Ben's tone, when he spoke, was calm and controlled. "The search-and-rescue team had already started out this morning," he said. "There'll probably be a mobilizing charge."

"I'll pay it," Connor said promptly. "I have some money saved."

"And we've lost a full day moving the cattle." Ben addressed his son like an adult, an equal, discussing business of interest to them both.

"I thought about that," Connor said. "I was hoping I could make up for it by working the rest of the summer on the ranch. Without pay, of course. I'm pretty good with the horses."

Ben nodded, his face serious. "I could use a good horse man."

"All right!" Connor beamed. "That'll be great!" He jumped up in excitement, but then sat back down. His smile faded and he took a deep breath. Obviously, there was something else he needed to discuss, some other decision he'd reached.

"I know you're not really too thrilled about this art thing," he said. "But I'm good, Dad, really good, and I want to go to this art college in California."

"Sounds like a fine idea," Ben said.

Connor's grin flashed again, but he contained it and went on. "I was also thinking, you just might be right about the ranch sort of being in my blood. I don't see any reason why being a rancher and being an artist have to be so—"

"Incompatible?"

"Yeah, incompatible."

"No reason at all," Ben agreed.

"That's what I was thinking. No reason at all." Connor stood. "I'll go tell the guys it's time to eat." He grabbed a piece of sausage from the platter by the stove and headed for the door.

Ben's voice stopped him. "Connor?"

"Yeah, Dad?"

"I love you."

Connor grinned self-consciously. "Love you, too." He flipped his bangs out of his eyes, then reached up to finger them. "You know, I think I need a haircut."

That night fireworks lit the sky, and the fact that they were two days late didn't lessen anyone's enjoyment of the celebration. They'd gathered all the spare chairs, the benches from the table and even the couch from the cabin, and dragged them outside to form a semi-circle around the clearing so that everyone had a comfortable place from which to watch. Harvey and Connor did the honors, lighting the firecrackers with the long wooden kitchen matches used to start the stove. They darted forward, held the match steady, then leaped back a safe distance as the rockets sizzled, sputtered, then shot into the air, spinning red, green and gold sparks that floated gently down like miniature falling stars, burning out before they reached the ground.

Ben hadn't let Connor's homecoming stop them from putting in a full day's work. They'd returned home tired but satisfied and everyone seemed in a carefree mood, ready to enjoy the delayed Fourth of July party. Maria hadn't spent a minute alone with Ben since they'd gone for water by the spring that morning, yet she sensed a subtle shift in their relationship. It was impossible for either of them to retreat to their chilly poles after the closeness they'd shared during

Connor's disappearance—but the reality that she would be returning to Phoenix in a few short days was always there between them.

Something else bothered Maria, too, and when she saw Ben get up and carry the cooler into the cabin, she seized the opportunity and followed him in.

The kitchen was quiet after the raucous cowboys and exploding fireworks outside and Maria suddenly felt silly standing there beside the table, waiting for Ben to notice her. He was bent over at the waist, reaching to the back of the refrigerator for the last of the beer. A mosquito settled on her arm and she slapped at it, a sharp gunshot of a sound.

"Hi, there." Ben straightened and smiled at her. He began to pull the cans from the plastic rings of a six-pack holder and drop them into the ice-filled cooler. "Quite a production, isn't it?"

"It's wonderful." Maria ran a fingernail along a deep scratch on the old tabletop and tucked her other hand into the pocket of her jeans. "Connor's having a great time."

"Yeah, he is. It's just like old times." Ben dumped the rest of the beer into the cooler, closed the lid and picked it up. "I'm glad you got a chance to see Connor like this before you left, like he used to be. He's a good kid."

There was no easy way to bring up what she wanted to say, but Maria thought that was as good an opening as any. "Ben, there's something I wanted to tell you." Her finger stopped its nervous run along the groove in the table.

He sat the cooler back on the floor and Maria heard the melting ice slosh against its plastic sides. His expectant look made her even more uncomfortable and her words came out in a rush. "You didn't give me a chance to say this last night, but I really wanted you to know that I don't think you've made a 'mess' of Connor. I didn't want to leave with you thinking that I thought—well, what you thought I thought..." Maria let the awkward jumble of words die out.

"Thank you," Ben said. "I made a hell of a lot of mistakes with Connor—I guess I'm a slow learner—but I seem to be on the right track now. I'm getting better." He let a silence grow while he studied her intently. "I guess the question now is, am I good enough?"

He meant good enough for her girls, Maria understood instantly. She answered without hesitation. "Yes," she said. "You're more than good enough—much more."

A flame leaped into Ben's eyes. He stepped around the cooler and reached out for her. But Maria stopped him with a shake of her head before he could touch her. "That was never the problem."

"What?" Ben frowned in puzzlement and let his hands fall to his sides. "If you aren't worried about me being a good father to Tina and Trisha, then why in God's name are you leaving? Why are you taking them away?"

There was torment in Ben's voice, and it twisted inside Maria. She was unable to stop herself from voicing her deepest fear. "What about when you don't want to be their father anymore, Ben?" she demanded. "What happens to them then?"

"What are you talking about? Why would I do that?"

"Why did David's father do that?" she whispered. "Why did my father do that?"

Ben looked as if he'd been slapped. "Not that again! All men are tarred with the same brush, is that it? Forever? No man *ever* gets another chance with you?"

"I thought I'd let it go—all the old hurts—I really thought I had. But don't you see? It's not me, it's the girls. How can I take that chance with them? How?" Her torment was so great, so obvious, that the anger seemed to drain from Ben.

"I don't know," he said wearily. He sat down on the top of the cooler, the only place to rest in the now chairless cabin. He ran a hand down his face, then lifted his eyes to

look at her. "I can't change what your father did, or what
your brother-in-law did. I can't *make* you trust me. Trust is
something that needs time."

"I can't give you that time." She swallowed hard and
forced the words through the tightness of her throat. "Every
minute the girls spend with you, they get that much more
attached. It will just make everything harder in the end."

An especially loud firecracker burst outside and invol-
untarily Maria's eyes were drawn to the window. Bright
pinpricks of light exploded in all directions, shattering the
darkness with brilliant color, then disappearing almost instantly, leaving only a memory of its glory. Maria closed her
eyes. The beautiful pattern remained burned on her eyelids
for the briefest moment, but no matter how tight she
squeezed them shut she couldn't hold on to the light.

Chapter Ten

A glowing Veronica ran out to meet their truck as they pulled up to the ranch house three days later, the baby balanced on one hip, a stack of envelopes clutched in her free hand.

"Look, Maria! Look what the mailman brought me," she crowed. "He made a special trip out here just to get them to me. Look!"

Maria scooted across the seat and followed Connor out of the truck. Veronica thrust the stack into her hands as soon as her feet hit the ground.

"They're from Roberto. Can you believe it?"

Maria shuffled quickly through the envelopes. They were all addressed to Veronica in her husband's handwriting. "What happened?"

"You've got to read this letter from the secretary where Roberto's working." Veronica reached for an envelope on top of the stack. She tried to open it and remove the piece of paper inside, but her movements were hampered by the baby in her arms.

"Here, let me take Ashley for you." Connor casually lifted the baby from Veronica's arms and settled her against his chest as if he'd carried babies all his life. "What?" he asked as the three adults stared at him openmouthed. "I'm not going to drop her or anything." Ashley squealed happily, grabbed one of Connor's fingers and started to chew on it. "See, she likes me."

Maria scanned the letter her sister handed her. "So Roberto was giving his letters to his foreman to take into town and mail, and when the foreman quit, this secretary found all these letters in his desk?"

Veronica nodded. "And all my letters to Roberto were unclaimed at the post office down there. I guess they moved to this new construction site way out in the middle of the desert somewhere so the foreman was supposed to run all the errands in town, take care of the mail, stuff like that— except he really went to the bar instead. Roberto was writing to me three times a week and I didn't even know it. Can you believe it!" Veronica bubbled with excitement. "There was no way he could get to a phone to find out why I wasn't writing him back. Poor darling, he sounded worried to death in his last letter. I just called the company's headquarters in Tucson and they said they'd get a message out to him for me."

Maria hugged Veronica tight, so happy to see her vibrant and smiling again. "I'm so happy for you." She looked at Ben over her sister's shoulder, but Ben was watching Connor play with the baby, such pride on his face that Maria felt tears sting her eyes.

"Come on," Veronica said. "The girls are dying to see you."

"What I'm dying for is a shower," Maria said, blinking quickly and forcing herself to smile. "I've had enough of bathing out of a bucket."

Veronica laughed and tried to take Ashley from Connor's arms. The baby was cooing, a lock of the boy's long bangs clutched in her chubby fingers. "Let go, sweetheart." Veronica pried the baby's hand open.

"Ouch," Connor protested. "Listen, why don't you just leave her with me for a while before you pull my hair out by the roots. You go reread your letters or something and I'll bring her to you when she gets fussy."

Veronica hesitated and looked uncertainly at Maria. Maria nodded her approval. "If you're sure you don't mind..."

"No problem." Connor started for the house, the baby on his hip. "Veronica?" He stopped. "Could I talk to you a minute?"

Veronica joined him on the steps and Maria and Ben left them alone.

Connor absently patted the baby on the back, screwing up his courage. "I'm glad everything worked out okay with your husband," he finally managed.

"Thanks. So am I."

"And I'm sorry I acted like such a jerk—about Ashley and all, I mean. She's a great baby."

Veronica smiled. "It was my fault. I shouldn't have let you think she was Maria's all that time."

Connor looked at the beautiful woman standing in front of him, only three years older but a lifetime more experienced. "Why did you?" he asked.

Veronica took a long time to answer. "I don't... It's hard to explain." She shrugged. "I liked the attention, of course. And maybe I had a little bit—just a little bit—of a crush on you."

Connor felt the blush tingle all the way to the roots of his hair. "Well, all right! Maybe a little one, huh?"

"Maybe."

Connor's embarrassed grin lit his face. "Come on, Ashley. Let's you and me go visit the horses. Maybe we can find one that'd like a sugar cube."

Veronica watched him disappear around the corner of the house, murmuring to the baby. "Yeow!" Connor's yell reached her as she started down the steps, letters clutched to her chest. "Man, I really need a haircut."

That evening after supper, Ben and Connor put the finishing touches on the red sports car. Connor took the children for endless rides up and down the long lane past the pond, not seeming to mind the churning dust that settled over the shiny red paint. Then they set to work on Maria's dilapidated station wagon, preparing it for the long trip back to Phoenix in the morning. They had decided that Connor would follow her down in his car to make sure she arrived safely. He wanted to pick up some extra personal items from his mother's house since he was going to be spending the rest of the summer at the ranch.

"It was sweet of Connor to take the kids for a ride like that," Maria told her mother as they folded clothes in the bedroom and laid them in the open suitcases on the bed. "They're pretty upset about leaving."

"Of course they are upset," Mrs. Romero said bluntly. "Forcing them to go back to Phoenix just because you and Señor Ben—"

"Mama—" Maria cut her mother off, a warning in her voice. She had firmly refused to answer any questions from her mother or sister regarding her decision to leave, and she knew Ben had done the same with Harvey and Connor.

"None of my business. I am not saying a word about it. It is your job—you can quit whenever you want." Her mother thumped across the floor to pull open another dresser drawer; the disapproving beat of her walking stick spoke volumes. "It is a good thing to see the boy getting along with his father, though. A very good thing. And he looks *muy guapo* now with that flip-flop hair out of his eyes."

Maria laughed. "Yes, he does. You gave him a great haircut, Mama." She leaned on an overflowing suitcase, using her weight to push the lid closed enough to latch it, then heaved the suitcase onto the floor.

"But I thought Señor Ben would be happier," Mrs. Romero said with a sideways glance at her daughter. "If everything is so good with his son, then why would he still walk around with the sick eyes and broken face? Hmm?"

Maria ignored her mother's hints for information. She picked up a box from the floor and dumped the children's underwear and socks into it. "Ben's fine, Mama. In fact, he's so proud of Connor he could burst." She fingered one of the baby's tiny T-shirts. "You should have seen him when Connor was missing. He blamed himself for all the problems between them. He cares so much." Maria let the pastel garment drop unnoticed into the box, her mind turned inward as she remembered the suffering on Ben's face the night at the cabin when he'd talked about his son.

She mentally shook herself and tucked a stray strand of dark hair behind her ear. "Anyway, I'm glad they got a second chance. It's all going to work out just fine."

They packed in silence for a few minutes, the thump of the walking stick or the closing of a drawer the only sound in the small bedroom as the two women filled an assortment of boxes and sacks with their family's possessions. The light was fading quickly and Maria turned on the lamp on the nightstand. She'd have to call for the children to come in soon and get ready for bed. It would be a long drive tomorrow—with a lot of time to think.

Maria had a number of things she didn't want to think about. Like the way they'd all been so sure Roberto had deserted his family.

"Mama," Maria began, troubled. "Doesn't it bother you that we were ready to condemn Roberto so fast?"

"What do you mean?"

"Well, it was the first thing that came to mind, remember? Veronica doesn't hear from him for a week and instead of worrying about an accident or trying to find out what happened, we immediately assume he's left her. What does that say about us?"

Her mother didn't even look up from her packing. "It says we are not naive children, but women who have lived— and loved—in this world."

"But is it really this world? Or have we created our own angry little world where we see everything twisted, crooked, inside out?"

Now her mother did meet her eyes, and the old woman's eyes were dark and calm and very sure. "I know what my world looks like, Maria. And what Linda's world looks like." She paused a moment. "Maybe yours is different."

Maybe it was, Maria thought. It was so tiring to hold on to all the old bitterness, the constant wariness, the neverending vigil against getting hurt. Her mother's armor was so thick by now it must exhaust her to carry it. Maybe her own armor had thickened to the point where it was almost more painful to bear than the hurt it was supposed to protect against. Or maybe she was simply looking for an excuse to run to Ben and throw herself in his arms and beg him to hold her forever.

No, she told herself firmly, sitting the overflowing box on the floor. No, leaving was the right thing to do. And as she straightened, an unexpected thought hit her a glancing blow, a thought so startling she snapped upright. Had her father convinced himself to leave in just this way? Had he firmly, righteously, told himself it was best for all concerned? Old memories, forgotten memories she'd hoped she'd never have to deal with again, flooded through her.

"Mama," Maria began, unable to stop herself, "I was wondering... Do you think Papa ever felt like Ben did? I mean, do you think he ever wanted a second chance like Ben did with Connor?" Her voice was wistful. "I wonder if he ever sat up one night and felt...I don't know, sad or maybe just wished things had been different..."

"Hmph," her mother snorted. "I would not be surprised. He always whined about missing his *chicas* in his letters—"

Maria froze. She stared at the woman across the bed. Mrs. Romero's dark skin had turned an unhealthy shade of gray. "What do you mean?" Maria asked carefully.

"Nothing."

"You said 'his letters'— *Papa's* letters?"

"I meant letter, maybe one letter. Maybe just a few letters, every once in a while."

"Wait a minute." What she was hearing was incomprehensible. Maria stared hard at her mother, but her mother refused to meet her eyes; her gnarled fingers frantically continued to fold clothes. "Are you saying that Papa wrote you letters? You've always told us you never heard a word from him since the night he left."

Mrs. Romero remained stubbornly silent.

"Mama!"

Her mother gave up. She dropped the shirt in her hand and sat down heavily on the side of the bed, as if her legs were unable to support this extra burden. She closed her eyes, grappling with some emotion that seemed to drain the energy from her. When she finally spoke, her voice was flat, resigned. "Your father sends each of you girls a card on your birthday, every year."

Maria struggled to understand. "Still?" she asked. "Even now?"

"It never stops. Three times a year, year after year." She gave a small, biting laugh. "It is strange how he never remembered your birthdays before he left."

Maria still could not believe what she was hearing. "Papa has sent us birthday cards every year for... for *twenty years*... and you never told us? Our father tried to keep in touch with us—and you never told us!" She felt sick; her stomach heaved as the very foundation her life was built on lurched and shifted into a foreign pattern she had no ability to comprehend. She sank to the floor amid the boxes. "Why? Why, Mama?"

"He had no right to send you anything," her mother answered, her eyes flashing back to life. "He had no right to buy some cheap card and a stamp once a year and say, here, this makes me your father. He had no right to give you hope—to make you think that some day you might see him again. He had *no right* to be your father after what he did to us."

Maria could only stare up at her mother. Her mind reeled with the effort to reconcile the twisted face of the woman before her with the strong, stalwart... survivor... she'd always known her mother to be.

"Stop looking at me like that," her mother commanded. "He was a weak man, nothing at all like my papa. He had nothing, *nothing,* to give his girls."

Maria pulled the flowered fabric of her skirt over her knees and hugged her knees to her chest, cradling herself

"Maybe we should have been allowed to be the judge of that," she said in a whisper.

The old woman's face sagged, visibly aging in the harsh light from the bedside lamp. "What was I supposed to do, Maria? Was I supposed to let him come back? What would happen to my babies when he decided to leave again?" Now she met her daughter's eyes, pleading for understanding. "Do you know what it was like to have to tell my precious angels that their father had left them? *Madre de Dios*, don't you remember what it did to you and Linda?"

Her voice cracked and tears began to course down the weathered creases in her cheeks. She held out a hand to Maria, beseeching. "Was I supposed to let him do that to you again?"

"Oh, Mama." Maria jumped up and threw herself onto the bed, wrapping her arms around her mother.

"Never, never would I let that man hurt my girls again!" Mrs. Romero held Maria with a fierce protectiveness as if the woman in her arms were still the nine-year-old girl she'd had to awaken the day after her birthday with the news that her father was gone. "Never. Never." She repeated the word over and over again.

Maria held her mother on the bed as the twilight deepened into darkness and the two women cried together for a long, long time.

Ben looked up at the sound of the knock on his office door. He hadn't really been working; the computer-generated sheet of figures on beef prices had been no more than a blur in front of his eyes. The only thought in his mind was of Maria. Maria—who didn't trust him not to hurt her and her children, and yet refused to give him the time to earn her trust. It was a paradox that Ben rejected. There was

an answer to every problem even if the answer had to b
wrestled to the ground and hog-tied against its will.

"Come in," Ben called in response to the knock. He'
promised Connor he'd play cards with him that evening.

But it wasn't his son who pushed open the office door
Instead, Maria stood outlined in the threshold. She looke
so beautiful Ben felt his breath catch painfully in his chest
Her long hair was disheveled around her shoulders, and sh
was barefoot beneath her flowered skirt and white blouse
as rare and fragile looking as a desert bloom.

But as she moved into the light, Ben could see her cheek
were streaked with tears. He was by her side in a heartbeat
"What is it?" he demanded. "What's wrong?"

Maria walked straight into his arms and he closed then
around her automatically. She was no longer crying, but sh
held very still, like a frightened animal seeking protection
Ben gathered her close and let the warmth of his body quie
the tiny tremors that passed through her. Slowly, his hand
and voice gentle, he lifted her chin so he could look into he
face. "Maria, what's the matter?"

Her voice was so small Ben had to strain to hear it
"Everything could have been different," she whispered with
a bleakness that tore at him, "if she'd been willing to giv
him another chance. I know he didn't deserve it, but..."

"Come here." Ben led her to the small leather sofa be
side his desk and pressed her down, then settled protec
tively next to her. He listened while, in a halting voice
choking on tears that tortured her throat, she told him wha
her mother had done.

"He wanted to be a part of our lives—even if it was jus
a tiny part," Maria said. "Maybe I would have still re
sented him, maybe I would have even hated him, but i
would have been nothing compared to how I've felt abou
him all these years."

Ben watched Maria's hands clench reflexively in her skirt, punching and twisting the fabric. "She didn't *know* he would hurt us, but she was so hurt herself, so angry, that she refused to let him have anything to do with us. She denied us the opportunity to make the decision for ourselves. Maybe we would have gotten hurt again, but maybe not—"

Ben laid a hand over Maria's restless fingers, stilling them. He gathered them to his chest and held them against his heart, hoping the calm beat of it would steady her.

Maria half turned and looked up into his face. "I always thought she was so strong and so brave and so wonderful, and she is—she really is—but she's also bitter and angry and even vengeful." Maria's eyes filled with despair. "And I'm exactly the same."

"No," Ben protested.

"Yes, I am. You were right about Mama passing it on to me and me passing it on to the girls. I was teaching Tina and Trisha to be suspicious of all men, to always keep their distance, to never leave themselves open—to be man-haters, or man-bashers, or whatever it was you called us."

Ben couldn't stand to see the look of self-condemnation on her face. He brought her fingers to his lips and kissed them. "Your mother only did what she felt she had to do to protect her children. Just like you're trying to protect yours."

"I know," Maria agreed. "But I've been trying to protect my children by turning my back on the man I love."

Ben stiffened as the impact of her words hit him with a force that made rational thought difficult. Warily, he searched her face for some sign of confirmation. "Maria?" He didn't give a damn if he sounded hesitant. The feel of her hand cupped against his cheek had his insides so churned up he couldn't be sure of anything.

"I love you, Ben. And I've been trying to tell myself that it doesn't matter, when, really, it's the only thing that does matter."

Ben jumped to his feet as adrenaline coursed through him. He pulled her up after him, wanting to feel the length of her body pressed against him as he kissed her. He showered her face, her lips, her eyes, with exultant kisses. "Say it again," he demanded.

"I love you."

"And you're going to stay?"

"As long as you'll have me."

Ben let out a shout and lifted Maria off her feet, swinging her around in a circle.

Maria laughed. "Tina's such a smart little girl," she said. "She knew a good man when she saw one—in spite of everything I've taught her. Tina was willing to take the risk, to love you, never mind the consequences."

"She's a genius," Ben agreed, twirling Maria around again.

"Ben, put me down," Maria gasped. "You're making me dizzy."

"Good. You've made me dizzy for the past month and a half."

"I'm serious. I want to tell you something."

She really did sound serious, and Ben felt a moment's dread. He let her feet touch the floor but refused to loosen his hold on her despite the little push she gave against his chest. Whatever she had to say, she'd say it without a safe distance between them.

"I love you, Ben, yet I panicked like crazy at the thought I'm so sorry if I hurt you. I—"

Ben silenced her with a long kiss. Then he took her by the shoulders, facing her squarely, intent on making himself clear. "I love you. I love your children. We're going to grow

ld together, very old, forever. I don't want to be the last of
dying breed anymore. We've got each other and this crazy
roup. We'll be the family of the year, every year, from now
n. Understand?''

Maria nodded, solemn, and offered her face for another
iss.

Ben obliged, and it was some moments before he raised
is head and sighed. "I guess I better go to work on the sta-
ion wagon, first thing in the morning then."

Maria looked at him questioningly. "I thought you and
Connor worked on it tonight."

"We did." Ben tried to sound casual, but he could tell by
he sudden suspicion in her eyes that he'd failed.

"What's the matter?" The suspicion was close to accu-
ation now.

"All right, you'll find out soon enough, anyway." Tak-
ng her by the hand, he guided her over to the corner of the
oom. He picked up a rug that covered two cardboard boxes
o reveal a jumble of greasy black engine parts.

"Ben!"

"I admit it, we stole the idea from you. But it was such a
ood idea, and it worked so well with Connor—"

"You took apart my car!"

"I had to do something to stop you from leaving," Ben
rotested, trying to control his smile. "I needed time—"

"Time?" Maria laughed with delight and threw her arms
round him. "We have forever, remember?"

And this time his kiss was a hot brand, the Calder brand,
marking her his for life.

Epilogue

It was early fall, but Phoenix was still blazingly hot and the runways at Sky Harbor Airport shimmered and wavered through the floor-to-ceiling windows of the arrival area. A large, noisy group of adults and children waited impatiently at the end of a carpeted ramp that led into the bowels of an airplane that had just pulled up to the gate. A dark-haired boy swung on the red velvet ropes that cordoned off the ramp from the rest of the room, making a long hallway for the arriving passengers to walk down.

A tall man, slightly stooped with age, thinning silver hair carefully combed, appeared at the top of the ramp. He used his cane sparingly as he made his way toward the lights and noise of the busy airport.

A tentative smile brightened his faded eyes as he spied the waving children. His grandchildren! He searched the smiling faces turned expectantly toward him. He recognized Linda immediately—and her little boy—a handsome, sturdy boy dressed in a striped shirt with a mischievous grin.

And there was little Veronica, the daughter he'd never seen. She was beautiful, he thought with a pang. Her arm was around a strong-looking young man who held a baby on his broad shoulders, unselfconsciously helping the child wave her tiny hand up and down at her approaching *abuelo*.

The letters he'd received all summer from his girls had been descriptive enough that he easily recognized the bent old cowboy in baggy jeans and the round-faced woman with smiling eyes as Harvey and Vergie, the newlyweds just back from a honeymoon in Colorado.

His eyes swept the faces again, looking for— Ah, there she was. Maria. His Maria, whose wedding he'd come to attend. She held tightly onto the arm of a big, suntanned man as if she needed his strength while tears streamed down her cheeks. He felt tears come to his own eyes, tears of joy at the thought of her holding his arm the same way tomorrow as he walked her down the aisle. He looked closely at the man by her side, discerned the strength of his jaw, the proud carriage of his shoulders, and was satisfied with what he saw. The boy, looking so much like the man, would be her stepson, and the two adorable girls would be Tina and Trisha.

A good family, he thought to himself. He leaned more heavily on his cane and tried to hurry down the never-ending ramp, impatient to reach his family. But he didn't have to wait. Ignoring the red velvet rope, the group surged toward him, surrounding him, enveloping him, loving and forgiving him.

*   *   *   *   *

COMING NEXT MONTH

#1198 MAD FOR THE DAD—Terry Essig
Fabulous Fathers
He knew next to nothing about raising his infant nephew. So
ingle "dad" Daniel Van Scott asked his lovely new neighbor
Rachel Gatlin for a little advice—and found himself noticing her
charms as both a mother...*and* as a woman.

#1199 HAVING GABRIEL'S BABY—Kristin Morgan
Bundles of Joy
One fleeting night of passion and Joelle was in the family way!
And now the father of her baby, hardened rancher Gabriel Lafleur,
insisted they marry immediately. But could they find true love
before their bundle of joy arrived?

#1200 NEW YEAR'S WIFE—Linda Varner
Home for the Holidays
Years ago, the man Julie McCrae had loved declared her too
young for him and walked out of her life. Now Tyler Jordan was
back, and Julie was all woman. But did she dare hope that Tyler
would renew the love they'd once shared, and make her his New
Year's Wife?

#1201 FAMILY ADDITION—Rebecca Daniels
Single dad Colt Wyatt thought his little girl, Jenny, was all he
needed in his life, until he met Cassandra Sullivan—the lovely
woman who enchanted his daughter and warmed his heart. But
after so long, would he truly learn to love again and make
Cassandra an addition to his family?

#1202 ABOUT THAT KISS—Jayne Addison
Maid of honor Joy Mackey was convinced that Nick Tremain was
out to ruin her sister's wedding. And she was determined to go to
any lengths to see her sis happily wed—even if it meant keeping
Nick busy by marrying him herself!

#1203 GROOM ON THE LOOSE—Christine Scott
To save him from scandal, Cassie Andrews agreed to pose as
Greg Lawton's *pretend* significant other. The handsome doctor
was surely too arrogant—and way too sexy—to be real husband
material! Or was this groom just waiting to be tamed?

FAST CASH 4031 DRAW RULES
NO PURCHASE OR OBLIGATION NECESSARY

Fifty prizes of $50 each will be awarded in random drawings to be conducted no later than 3/28/97 from amongst all eligible responses to this prize offer received as of 2/14/97. To enter, follow directions, affix 1st-class postage and mail OR write Fast Cash 4031 on a 3" x 5" card along with your name and address and mail that card to: Harlequin's Fast Cash 4031 Draw, P.O. Box 1395, Buffalo, NY 14240-1395 OR P.O. Box 618, Fort Erie, Ontario L2A 5X3. (Limit: one entry per outer envelope; all entries must be sent via 1st-class mail.) Limit: one prize per household. Odds of winning are determined by the number of eligible responses received. Offer is open only to residents of the U.S. (except Puerto Rico) and Canada and is void wherever prohibited by law. All applicable laws and regulations apply. Any litigation within the province of Quebec respecting the conduct and awarding of a prize in this sweepstakes maybe submitted to the Régie des alcools, des courses et des jeux. In order for a Canadian resident to win a prize, that person will be required to correctly answer a time-limited arithmetical skill-testing question to be administered by mail. Names of winners available after 4/28/97 by sending a self-addressed, stamped envelope to: Fast Cash 4031 Draw Winners, P.O. Box 4200, Blair, NE 68009-4200.

OFFICIAL RULES
MILLION DOLLAR SWEEPSTAKES
NO PURCHASE NECESSARY TO ENTER

1. To enter, follow the directions published. Method of entry may vary. For eligibility, entries must be received no later than March 31, 1998. No liability is assumed for printing errors, lost, late, non-delivered or misdirected entries.
   To determine winners, the sweepstakes numbers assigned to submitted entries will be compared against a list of randomly pre-selected prize winning numbers. In the event all prizes are not claimed via the return of prize winning numbers, random drawings will be held from among all other entries received to award unclaimed prizes.

2. Prize winners will be determined no later than June 30, 1998. Selection of winning numbers and random drawings are under the supervision of D. L. Blair, Inc., an independent judging organization whose decisions are final. Limit: one prize to a family or organization. No substitution will be made for any prize, except as offered. Taxes and duties on all prizes are the sole responsibility of winners. Winners will be notified by mail. Odds of winning are determined by the number of eligible entries distributed and received.

3. Sweepstakes open to residents of the U.S. (except Puerto Rico), Canada and Europe who are 18 years of age or older, except employees and immediate family members of Torstar Corp., D. L. Blair, Inc., their affiliates, subsidiaries, and all other agencies, entities, and persons connected with the use, marketing or conduct of this sweepstakes. All applicable laws and regulations apply. Sweepstakes offer void wherever prohibited by law. Any litigation within the province of Quebec respecting the conduct and awarding of a prize in this sweepstakes must be submitted to the Régie des alcools, des courses et des jeux. In order to win a prize, residents of Canada will be required to correctly answer a time-limited arithmetical skill-testing question to be administered by mail.

4. Winners of major prizes (Grand through Fourth) will be obligated to sign and return an Affidavit of Eligibility and Release of Liability within 30 days of notification. In the event of non-compliance within this time period or if a prize is returned as undeliverable, D. L. Blair, Inc. may at its sole discretion award that prize to an alternate winner. By acceptance of their prize, winners consent to use of their names, photographs or other likeness for purposes of advertising, trade and promotion on behalf of Torstar Corp., its affiliates and subsidiaries, without further compensation unless prohibited by law. Torstar Corp. and D. L. Blair, Inc., their affiliates and subsidiaries are not responsible for errors in printing of sweepstakes and prizewinning numbers. In the event a duplication of a prizewinning number occurs, a random drawing will be held from among all entries received with that prizewinning number to award that prize.

SWP-S12ZD1

5. This sweepstakes is presented by Torstar Corp., its subsidiaries and affiliates in conjunction with book, merchandise and/or product offerings. The number of prizes to be awarded and their value are as follows: Grand Prize — $1,000,000 (payable at $33,333.33 a year for 30 years); First Prize — $50,000; Second Prize — $10,000; Third Prize — $5,000; 3 Fourth Prizes — $1,000 each; 10 Fifth Prizes — $250 each; 1,000 Sixth Prizes — $10 each. Values of all prizes are in U.S. currency. Prizes in each level will be presented in different creative executions, including various currencies, vehicles, merchandise and travel. Any presentation of a prize level in a currency other than U.S. currency represents an approximate equivalent to the U.S. currency prize for that level, at that time. Prize winners will have the opportunity of selecting any prize offered for that level; however, the actual non U.S. currency equivalent prize, if offered and selected, shall be awarded at the exchange rate existing at 3:00 P.M. New York time on March 31, 1998. A travel prize option, if offered and selected by winner, must be completed within 12 months of selection and is subject to: traveling companion(s) completing and returning a Release of Liability prior to travel; and hotel and flight accommodations availability. For a current list of all prize options offered within prize levels, send a self-addressed, stamped envelope (WA residents need not affix postage) to: MILLION DOLLAR SWEEPSTAKES Prize Options, P.O. Box 4456, Blair, NE 68009-4456, USA.

6. For a list of prize winners (available after July 31, 1998) send a separate, stamped, self-addressed envelope to: MILLION DOLLAR SWEEPSTAKES Winners, P.O. Box 4459, Blair, NE 68009-4459, USA.

EXTRA BONUS PRIZE DRAWING
NO PURCHASE OR OBLIGATION NECESSARY TO ENTER

7. The Extra Bonus Prize will be awarded in a random drawing to be conducted no later than 5/30/98 from among all entries received. To qualify, entries must be received by 3/31/98 and comply with published directions. Prize ($50,000) is valued in U.S. currency. Prize will be presented in different creative expressions, including various currencies, vehicles, merchandise and travel. Any presentation in a currency other than U.S. currency represents an approximate equivalent to the U.S. currency value at that time. Prize winner will have the opportunity of selecting any prize offered in any presentation of the Extra Bonus Prize Drawing; however, the actual non U.S. currency equivalent prize, if offered and selected by winner, shall be awarded at the exchange rate existing at 3:00 P.M. New York time on March 31, 1998. For a current list of prize options offered, send a self-addressed, stamped envelope (WA residents need not affix postage) to: Extra Bonus Prize Options, P.O. Box 4462, Blair, NE 68009-4462, USA. All eligibility requirements and restrictions of the MILLION DOLLAR SWEEPSTAKES apply. Odds of winning are dependent upon number of eligible entries received. No substitution for prize except as offered. For the name of winner (available after 7/31/98), send a self-addressed, stamped envelope to: Extra Bonus Prize Winner, P.O. Box 4463, Blair, NE 68009-4463, USA.

SWP-S12ZD2

The collection of the year!
NEW YORK TIMES BESTSELLING AUTHORS

Linda Lael Miller
Wild About Harry

Janet Dailey
Sweet Promise

Elizabeth Lowell
Reckless Love

Penny Jordan
Love's Choices

and featuring
Nora Roberts
The Calhoun Women

This special trade-size edition features four of the wildly popular titles in the Calhoun miniseries together in one volume—a true collector's item!

Pick up these great authors and a chance to win a weekend for two in New York City at the Marriott Marquis Hotel on Broadway! We'll pay for your flight, your hotel—even a Broadway show!

Available in December at your favorite retail outlet.

NEW YORK
Marriott®
MARQUIS

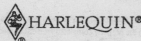

As seen on TV!
Free Gift Offer

With a Free Gift proof-of-purchase from any Silhouette® book,
you can receive a beautiful cubic zirconia pendant.

This gorgeous marquise-shaped stone is a genuine cubic
zirconia—accented by an 18" gold tone necklace.

(Approximate retail value $19.95)

Send for yours today…
compliments of ▼ *Silhouette*®

To receive your free gift, a cubic zirconia pendant, send us one original proof-of-
purchase, photocopies not accepted, from the back of any Silhouette Romance™,
Silhouette Desire®, Silhouette Special Edition®, Silhouette Intimate Moments®
or Silhouette Yours Truly™ title available in August, September, October, November and
December at your favorite retail outlet, together with the Free Gift Certificate, plus a
check or money order for $1.65 U.S./$2.15 CAN. (do not send cash) to cover postage and
handling, payable to Silhouette Free Gift Offer. We will send you the specified gift. Allow
6 to 8 weeks for delivery. Offer good until December 31, 1996 or while quantities last.
Offer valid in the U.S. and Canada only.

Free Gift Certificate

Name: _____

Address: _____

City: _____ State/Province: _____ Zip/Postal Code: _____

Mail this certificate, one proof-of-purchase and a check or money order for postage
and handling to: SILHOUETTE FREE GIFT OFFER 1996. In the U.S.: 3010 Walden
Avenue, P.O. Box 9077, Buffalo NY 14269-9077. In Canada: P.O. Box 613, Fort Erie,
Ontario L2Z 5X3.

FREE GIFT OFFER   084-KMD
ONE PROOF-OF-PURCHASE

To collect your fabulous FREE GIFT, a cubic zirconia pendant, you must include this
original proof-of-purchase for each gift with the properly completed Free Gift Certificate.

084-KMD-R

FORTUNE'S Children™

Bestselling Author
ARLENE
JAMES

Continues the twelve-book series—FORTUNE'S CHILDREN—
in **December 1996** with Book Six

SINGLE WITH CHILDREN

Handsome widower Adam Fortune desperately needed help raising
his three small children. So he hired lovely Laura Beaumont as their
live-in nanny. Could Laura overcome her past so they could become
the family she'd always dreamed of?

MEET THE FORTUNES—a family whose legacy is greater than riches.
Because where there's a will…there's a *wedding!*

A CASTING CALL TO
ALL FORTUNE'S CHILDREN FANS!
If you are truly fortunate,
you may win a trip to
Los Angeles to audition for
Wheel of Fortune®. Look for
details in all retail Fortune's Children titles!

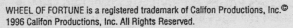

Look us up on-line at: http://www.romance.net   FC-6-C

You're About to
Become a
Privileged
Woman

**Reap the rewards of fabulous free gifts and
benefits with proofs-of-purchase from
Silhouette and Harlequin books**

Pages & Privileges™

**It's our way of thanking you for
buying our books at your
favorite retail stores.**

**PROOF OF
PURCHASE**
SR-PP20
Offer expires March 31, 1997

Harlequin and Silhouette—
the most privileged readers in the world!

**For more information about Harlequin and
Silhouette's PAGES & PRIVILEGES program call the
Pages & Privileges Benefits Desk: 1-503-794-2499**

Silhouette®

SR-PP20